A Tale of Two Wives

Stephanie Castle

"THE CASCADE SERIES"

PERCEPTIONS PRESS

Vancouver, B.C.

A Tale of Two Wives

National Library of Canada Cataloguing in Publications

Castle, Stephanie
A tale of two wives / Stephanie Castle.

(The cascade series)
ISBN 0-9734293-4-8

1. Title. II. Series: Castle, Stephanie Cascade series

PS8555.A7857T34 2004 C813'.54 C2004-902272-5

Typesetting by Ten Plus Productions
Burnaby, BC

Published by Perceptions Press
8415 Granville St.
Box 46
Vancouver, BC V6P 4Z9

Cover Design: Pat Monty

Printed in Canada

TABLE OF CONTENTS

Books by **Stephanie Castle** *in this Genre*

Fiction

TALES FROM CASCADIA

THE PARTNERSHIP

THE DUAL ALLIANCE

SHADOWS IN THE CITY

Non-fiction

FEELINGS
A Transsexual's Explanation of a Baffling Condition

PRISONER OF GENDER
A Transsexual and the System
(with Katherine Johnson)

PREFACE

Dealing with relationships presents a transsexual with one of the biggest challenges imaginable in charting a new course through the life ahead. Having, after much vacillation and uncertainty, decided to face the fact that he* is transsexual and to deal with the condition positively, he has to develop new relationships, adjust older ones and, in some instances, write off some that might be greatly cherished. He has to dispose of much of the baggage of a former life at the same time as he picks up and adjusts to a whole new set of ground rules with all their social implications.

A man becoming a woman, or vice versa, can reasonably anticipate entrenched prejudices impinging on his family and social life. His workplace role may also be grievously affected. But no matter what the extent of change there will be a host of lesser, often very subtle, challenges to face. For example, a man who never felt any barrier going unaccompanied into a pub or bar might feel inhibited if he did the same thing as a woman. As a new woman "she" will feel the vulnerability into which women have been cast in their social and sexual role for hundreds of generations. As a new woman she will feel the limitations placed on her new role even, in many instances, from her friends who either lack

* For convenience the musculine gender is used in this preface. The condition applies also to women wishing to become men.

the confidence, or simply do not know how to handle a social hot potato. And as a new woman she will experience the exercise of prejudice, often very subtle, without the prejudiced parties even knowing why they are prejudiced.

Transsexualism usually carries with it a high social cost. A surprisingly large number of transsexuals come from the ranks of married heterosexual men, a possible majority in fact. So it can hardly be surprising that marital breakup and its consequences on wives and children can be destructive. Unfortunately, the one who shoulders the blame is the transsexual person. He is tarred with a variety of brushes, few of which are flattering, but in a supportive understanding relationship the road ahead will be a lot easier on all concerned.

More than ever, a confused biological origin established in the fetal stage of development is recognized as the root cause of transsexualism. It is not something with which the sufferer from the condition is ever pleased to be afflicted. The only thing he can ever feel glad about is when he has dealt with it, perhaps with a sense of relief similar to any patient's satisfaction after coming through a serious illness. Nor does he learn to be a transsexual, for it is an unteachable subject. Yet there are people who are only too prepared to believe that exposure of a child to a transsexual may result in the child also developing the same "disease." Nothing could be further from the truth. It is not a transmittable disease. In fact, it is not a disease at all, but in its worst form it can lead to a serious psychological illness, which left untreated might lead to other medical conditions, such as heart and other problems growing out of stress and anxiety. His behaviour while reacting to these might include personal neglect and a variety of irresponsible acts and even suicide in some cases.

How do people react when they are first told of the condition in someone they love or know very well? The most predictable response is denial – to shut one's ears and close one's eyes to it, and to pretend that by ignoring it, it will go away. It will not go away, because it is a lifetime condition with which one is born. If dealt with adequately a subject can live with it happily enough and even reshape his life so much that he is, in effect, a reborn person perhaps much improved over the old biological shell from which he sprang.

For the "new" woman, self-confidence is more critical than perfect feminine features, a flawless feminine voice, a great figure and all the other accoutrements of a fine female presentation. Look around; feminine beauty which is certainly the dream of many transsexuals, is seldom fully attainable by the majority of biological women. If beauty is their objective it is invariably accompanied by compromise. If the transsexual can accept this premise and work with confidence and full acceptance that compromise applies equally to her as with her genetic sisters, then she can enjoy a happy and fulfilling life in her new role.

If confidence is not there then she will spend far too much of her life worrying about passing, looking over her shoulder always with a guilt-ridden conscience. Unfortunately, the blooming of self-confidence in a person undergoing treatment is not always predictable. Surgical procedures are one barometer of success, but if the spirit and confidence are absent or diminished then the new role will be capable of generating great discomfort.

The role of a supportive family is critical at all times. Regrettably, it is not always available. Too often the first reaction is unaccommodating and in some instances even violent. Hence the chances of a sound, well-oriented, self-confident gender-changed person are undermined. The agony that this can pile on to an already fragile person is beyond comprehension.

In this story the theme is foretold by the title. The comparison is made between two intertwining cases with similar economic and educational backgrounds and how the two wives involved handled their husband's transition. One was foolish and unreasoning which contributed to her transsexual husband's ruin. The other showed wisdom and a substantial element of humanity and compassion and the result speaks for itself in the narrative.

By acting the characters out, what follows will hopefully explain the condition and create a better basis for understanding and provide some answers to a mystery as perplexing as the human mind can grapple with. If the condition appears to be one of mistaken sex differentiation while in the womb, it is also one often associated with social destruction, financial ruin and a host of other evils. It is doubtful if the condition can ever be fully understood, even by the most competent of medical people. Until one lives it, its tragedy, its pain, its pathos, the beauty of rebirth which some experience, its emotional moments and even its shades of humour, it is difficult if not impossible, to relate, to convey or to adequately describe to others.

In short, it's a patchwork quilt, a crazy mosaic, a labyrinth of conflicts, ideas and emotional feelings. If one can find one's way through this jungle there is hope for a decent, less complex future at the end of the road. Unfortunately there are those who lose their way and for them the end result is at best continuing unhappiness, at worst the possibility of suicide.

Part I

The Tragedy

Chapter One

Gloomy Sunday

David Rakewood sat in his car overlooking the sea. He was parked at one of those viewpoints so beloved by tourists. Beneath was a drop of several hundred feet. In his moments of depression he had contemplated jumping over the parapet to the rocks below, or even in a moment of greater madness, driving his car at high speed through the barrier in the hope that he could encompass his own destruction in one great spectacular gesture of giving up on life.

David was still precariously hanging on to a business career for which in earlier years he had entertained high hopes. A few years ago he had been recognized as a man with great leadership potential in the business community. He was one who would always support a good cause with his cheque book when he was in agreement with its aims. His company was prosperous and well respected, but others of necessity were taking over management. This was to ensure its survival because over the past two or three years he had become neglectful and his dependence on the bottle was causing a loss of personal respect all round. More and more he was becoming the boss in name only. Even when he was sober, he was frequently listless and lacked the will to deal with anything positively. His personality was a perfect incubator for the alcoholic condition.

His problems of more recent times had included public scenes so bad that he had been written off by some as a "drunk". He'd seen the breakup of his marriage, a near total estrangement from his children, and his banishment from his own beautiful home into which he had poured his heart and energies, and had planned and saved.

He had asked himself a thousand times why he had been dealt such a poor hand by the circumstances of his life. He had always been perceived by the outside world as a "comer," a man destined for greater things. In short, he had been a modern success story, a good education, an excellent business career, a nice home and a beautiful wife and fine children. What else could a normal, average man wish for? David knew the answer to his own questions, but was unable to face up to the facts of his own life. In moments of honesty with himself he knew he was alcoholic but he was unable to see that a personality flaw was part of his problem. He did tend to blame everyone else for the problems his drinking had created, but yet he knew when he was able to be honest with himself, that everything he now did was a matter of running away from life.

But for David there had always been another side to him that until recently he had hidden, denied, and fervently hoped that he would never have to reveal to anyone. So long as this influence in his life could be suppressed and hidden he could continue to lead the life of an apparently normal man even if he had a drinking problem, accepted by his peers and those people in his life who were important to him, including his wife and children.

This influence, this unseen presence with which David had grown up, had shared his mind as though at times another person resided there. He had heard the common statement that there is something of our opposite sex in all of us. He accepted the truth of that but, unlike an unaffected person who could quickly dismiss the thought from his mind like discarding a soiled paper napkin, the thought in David's case seldom was out of his mind. When it was, a chance remark or a tiny circumstance could bring it back with renewed force.

He came to accept that this strange, indescribable, almost mystical feeling he first felt in his early childhood had gradually developed a distinct presence within him. He came to recognize the presence as his highly developed, highly sensitive female personality, sometimes comforting, often demanding because she had no consideration for his convenience when she chose the time to make her presence felt. Sometimes he liked her and welcomed her presence for the extra dimensions she seemed to add to his life. At other times he fiercely resented the way that she just seemed to barge into his daily scenes affecting his relationships, weakening his libido, undermining his conventional sense of security and encircling him like the coils of a snake.

He would fight back, exhausting himself in the process, leaving him stressed out and in a state of deep anxiety. He knew and appreciated the statement so often made by transsexuals, that he felt like a woman trapped in a man's body. When that point was reached he would wonder if life was worth living. To drown his sorrows he would go on a bender.

When his final crisis came, when all the visible influences in his life and the unseen forces within him converged, he finally realized that he had to face this presence and accept the consequences of all the circumstances "she" created. It was either that or see whatever remained of his life in ruins, unrepaired, unfulfilled and deeply disturbed. This is what had brought him to the brink of self-destruction, had all but destroyed his married and family life, and brought on the nagging thought that he must start afresh, chart a new course, rebuild from the ground up, and that this way he could start to enjoy the happiness that he knew should rightfully be his.

David Rakewood was a transsexual. He had grown up with great sensitivities which can create a crisis out of normal enough circumstances. He had been burdened with repressions unknown to an unaffected person and in order to hide all this he became a consummate and perpetual actor who eventually became disgusted with the lack of self-truth in his life. He knew the price of change was high, but when the pressure for transition became unbearable, he had to recognize the alternatives.

In the final analysis he concluded that for family, social and business reasons, this unseen but fully-felt force within him must be rejected. For him there was only one remaining course of action that seemed possible. This was the one where he considered driving his car at high speed over the cliff. This latter prospect was frightening, but there were times when it seemed the only choice. This was one of those days, a typical West Coast rainy, misty and gloomy Sunday in its early hours before there was much traffic around, when the pulse of the world seemed to be at its slowest and quietest, when others securely slept in their beds. But for the tormented, like David, there seldom seemed to be any real rest at any time of any day. David looked at the Spanish moss hanging in shards from the nearby cedar trees which gave them a ghostlike appearance. The mist that seemed to trail from it, gave him a shudder. It all seemed so natural and yet it felt as though he was the sole occupant of a stage, a sort of setting for his own personal Valkyrie as she hovered there maybe awaiting him for the next world.

David started to feel drowsy under the warming influence of the Scotch whisky which he drank from a hip flask. He thought of the warm marital bed with Kathy laying there by herself, probably as lonely as he was, but too proud to admit it. She was a strange one in the view of many people, but to David who had fallen head-over-heels in love with her, she remained an enigma. She had been born with a golden spoon in her mouth and had been richly endowed by nature with the classic beauty of a Nefertiti or Cleopatra, but with it all went an egocentric personality, selfish and unfeeling to an extreme and at other times quite the opposite when it suited her purpose. Notwithstanding her natural beauty, he also wryly thought of the big bills for expensive and fashionable clothes, beauty treatments and hair-dos that came in with uncommon frequency. He paid most of them, but when he protested she paid them from her own inheritance as if to remind him that she had independent means quite beyond his own. It was a bone of contention between them.

David's alcohol-sodden mind drifted to his two surviving children. Elaine, the only daughter with whom he always had a close relationship, was also a rebel in terms of the Rakewood's life style. Even though her parents provided her with a comfortable home, she always deprecated wealth and spoke in favour of the poverty-stricken. Even though David loved his 18-year old daughter dearly he had to admit to himself that she was a contradiction, probably as screwed up in her own particular way as his wife. Alan on the other hand at 16 years of age and as handsome as his mother was beautiful was doing well at school and had been talking with David up until recent times about his son's career choices. Alan, who had inherited something of his mother's arrogance, seemed uncertain as to what he wanted to do so David had suggested that he take an arts degree at university while he explored his options. In his imagination his eye wandered onto the picture of little Jimmy, the youngest child who had died of cancer at the early age of six. That death seemed to mark the point when Kathy and David started to drift apart and he wondered why.

He thought of the plant, noisy and smokey down on the assembly deck where welders worked away fabricating all manner of steel assemblies. He had learned to weld there, as his father insisted that if he was to one day take over the plant, he had to know every stage of its operations. There was something vaguely comforting about the smell of burning metal and the gas given off in the welding process. It had a mildly acrid smell which was not unpleasant. It was as familiar to him as the pleasant odour of coffee and bacon with eggs. He thought of men on the welding floor who once knew him as Dave, but now addressed him as

"Mr. Rakewood, Sir." After all it was the respect due to him as the employer, but he knew it was phoney and he told himself that he could detect the mockery in their voices. Did they really respect him and what had he done to earn their respect after stepping out of his welding clothes and into the executive suite?

He used to be happy with his thoughts as he worked away with a torch and welding rod. At the end of the day he knew he had achieved something that gave him satisfaction, but now he had to be nursed along by his fellow executives. Harry Austin, his financial vice-president would sit down and explain the financial state of the firm and he would nod assent to almost anything he heard. After all, he trusted Harry who had served his father before him and he also knew that Harry was too much of a faithful servant and gentlemen to ever prick David's ego by revealing the depth of his ignorance.

Jake Early was another member of the executive and in many ways now the real captain of the ship who, as executive vice-president, would take over from David if anything should ever happen to him. Jake was abrasive at times and had difficulty in hiding the contempt he occasionally felt for David. At other times Jake liked David, but did not really respect his boss who he also knew was now just not up to the job and was in fact holding the company back. Jake was the first management type to come up from the shop floor and in the early years of their association he knew David for the dynamic, energetic and very clever guy who never let any grass grow under his feet. Jake could see the damage alcohol was doing to his boss and knew it was only a matter of time before drink finally got hold of David and destroyed him.

David's thoughts turned to the starkly modern apartment he was now renting while he tried to sort out his tangled life. The place was cold and lifeless. It felt too much like many an hotel room of the type he had often stayed in while on business trips and to add to his discomfort he was not a good housekeeper. He was alone in a darkened car with his troubled thoughts. Maybe tomorrow would be a better day when he returned to the hustle and bustle of his office and the fabricating plant. He took another swig of the whisky which helped him relax as he sat behind the wheel of his car and dropped off into a troubled sleep.

In the quiet of the night, the rain beat an insistent drumbeat on the roof. It provided an accompaniment to David's deep snores as his chest lifted and fell in cadence. He was awakened after an hour or two of slumber. His mouth felt horrible and the whisky bottle lay empty and lifeless on the floor. He needed to urinate, grabbed the empty bottle and got out of the car letting his water run freely on the grass at the edge of the road. The bottle was flung in a graceful arc into the nearby trees. He climbed back into the driver's seat started the car and set an uncertain course back for his apartment, hoping along the way that he would not be spotted by a police patrol.

Chapter Two

A Tragedy Occurs

David Rakewood's grandfather, Theodore Rakosy, had come to Vancouver as a poor immigrant from Austria-Hungary, but by dint of hard work and the establishment of strong political and business connections he thrived as a brewer of some of the best beers produced in Canada.

David's father, Henry, had inherited the business before the First World War, but lacked the foresight and drive of his father. Being highly class-conscious he saw the need to anglicize the family name to Rakewood as a first step to entering the predominant Anglo-society which dominated the affairs of the city and province. The business fell into difficulties and was only saved by the advent of Prohibition in the United States, an act which created many millionaires in Canada. In the case of the Rakewoods, this prosperity while others suffered assured David and his two sisters of a good education and a comfortable upbringing. This was during the Depression of the '30s when brewers, distillers and anyone else who could turn out a good brew could sell everything they produced.

David went to university and gained his degree in structural engineering. When his father died suddenly, the family was left in far poorer condition than they had been led to believe. David shelved the idea of working towards his Ph.D. in engineering as there seemed to be more urgent matters to take his attention, including seeing to the comfort and security of his mother and the welfare of his two sisters. After the brewery was sold off one of the assets remaining was the old machine shop where a small crew headed by Jake Early dealt with the brewery's needs in the way of maintenance and repairs to machinery and equipment. It also was doing some outside work when David worked there as an apprentice welder while going through university. By dipping into what little family capital was available to him, he saw the opportunity of taking advantage of the buoyant postwar economy. He purchased the small plant from the estate and decided to enter the steel fabricating and construction business full time and very soon his infant company, Rakewood Fabricators Ltd., was making excellent progress.

He had known Kathy Lawrence for some years through his two sisters, all of whom went to the same girls' private school. The mutual attraction grew and eventually they were married in one of the city's bigger society weddings. David was remembered as the grandson of Theodore Rakosy, the successful immigrant brewer and son of millionaire Henry Rakewood, even if no one cared to enshrine the family's success in the days of bootlegged liquor into polite local history. Kathy was a daughter of one of the city's premier wealthy old families with a web of impeccable connections throughout the country's political and commercial elite.

David had everything going for him and the invitations to a variety of social functions came in a steady succession. An ambitious young businessman with his head screwed on tightly, he could not fail to profit as his business mushroomed on fat and profitable contracts. When any business was singled out by business magazines as being an example of a local success story, Rakewood Fabricators Ltd., the darling of the business establishment, was usually at the head of the pack.

Kathy was also the beneficiary of much reflected glory, being invited on to various charity committees or boards of the type which fawned over the wealthy and well-connected for what they could bring, quite beyond their ordinary human presence. Society magazines and "Talk of the Town" gossip columnists loved to get hold of copy like this, much of it shallow and basically meaningless to the ordinary citizen. But for those who frequented these pathways of society there was a sort of understanding that they, at least to themselves if to no one else, represented the "creme de la creme". The established nobility required as its conditions of entry, good connections, good breeding, an education at the right schools, membership in clubs favoured by the rich and powerful and a ready cheque-book when it came time to send ostentatious signals which let the world know one had "arrived." This was a crowd which judged as marks of personal success the neighbourhood where one lived, what type of car one drove, the location of one's summer cottage and the size of one's boat moored among the best berths down at the most prestigious of the local yacht clubs.

The marriage prospered and in fairly rapid succession a girl was followed by two younger brothers. But one cloud existed like a perpetual shadow on David's personal horizon. He was transsexual and had been aware of its presence since early childhood. His guilty secret had only been breached once, at about 13, causing much consternation in the family. This was when his mother discovered evidence of crossdressing and took him to the family doctor who dismissed it as something he would grow out of.

How wrong the doctor was. David took this as a warning of what he could expect in future if he was again discovered. Consequently he hid his shame, took his condition underground and redoubled his wariness of discovery. He devised ways and means by which he could enjoy his secret hobby of crossdressing. He kept a locked suitcase in a closet at his office in which he hid his collection of clothing and cosmetics. Sometimes when he travelled on a sales trip he would take his case and switch gender roles in the privacy of his hotel bedroom. He maintained a diary in which he expressed his sorrows, dissatisfactions and supreme loneliness. At times he enthused about his secret liking and at other times he became deeply ashamed and guilt-ridden. In short he derived satisfaction from being a secret crossdresser, but also suffered severe self-recrimination.

David's marriage to Kathy and the arrival of a family seemed to greatly pacify his innermost urgings and strengthen the marriage as the two settled into the role of parents. For several years, particularly while they added to their growing family, David was happy in the role of father. Kathy had a great beauty, but an icicle-like personality which seemed by its brittle coldness to repel David who had a great need for emotional warmth in order to fully express himself. At times she seemed like a confectionery doll glittering inside a see-through cellophane wrapper. She could be seen, but would not allow herself to be touched. Once pregnant with their first-born she seemed to thaw out and become warm and human again.

David's two younger sisters thought the world of their brother. Since the death of their father he had taken the role of head of the family. Helen, the eldest, was an economist with a major bank. She saw her brother very occasionally as she had lived in Toronto for years. The younger, with a warm and engaging personality, was Elizabeth. She was married with a family, and lived quite comfortably on the west side of the city with her stockbroker husband.

Tom Sadler, Elizabeth's husband, looked after Rakewood family investment accounts. The Sadlers had little use for Kathy, whom they regarded as a snob. Kathy in turn did her best to cut out the Sadlers from the Rakewood's social life, but this was always nullified by David's insistence on maintaining a close and warm friendship with his youngest sister and husband. When he wanted to relax he would often drift around to their comfortable and modest home for coffee or a beer with Tom. The reverse seldom took place as Kathy made it clear that the welcome mat was not usually out.

A severe unsettling setback occurred when the Rakewood's youngest child, six-year old Jimmy, died of cancer. This brought home to David just how precarious life really is. He suffered a series of depressions which brought back all his old unsettling gender identity memories and experiences.

His relationship with Kathy suffered because of his inability to adequately communicate, to get through to her. Normal marital debate was very limited as her mind was usually made up like a steel trap. Her views and pronouncements on life became unseen or implied barriers. He never knew her to express compassion for anyone in an inferior position, but she idolized those who seemed to have a superior social standing in her views and values of life. It was this atmosphere which left him feeling very lonely at times. He could not bury himself in his work at all hours of the day. At this point he had not become a heavy drinker, but he did feel very frustrated and felt she had been mocking in her periodic putting down of him.

One day David picked up a giveaway copy of the local underground newspaper, more out of curiosity than for any specific need. His attention was drawn to ads in the personal columns in which prostitutes, call girls and massage parlours offered a variety of services, all kinky, a few bizarre and some quite laughable. For some with desperate needs these offerings were taken very seriously and a good practitioner with a select clientele could make a very good living off the trade in unhappy, frustrated and disturbed souls.

One such ad had the exaggerated silhouette of a statuesque female. Ramona offered her range of services as a post-operative transsexual who had completed the surgical process of becoming a woman. She could provide makeovers, dressups, bondage, massage and whatever else the customer was prepared to pay for. On a whim David picked up his phone at the office after everyone else had gone home and called the number advertised. A husky, not unpleasant voice answered the phone with a throaty "Hullo." David asked for Ramona and the reply came through, "This is she speaking."

More than anything, David needed someone he could talk to who had an understanding of transsexualism. As the phone conversation carried on for a few minutes he became quite desperate to meet Ramona.

"Whatever your rate is, I'm quite prepared to pay. I just want to be able to cross-dress and talk to someone. Crossdressing is not new to me, but I've never yet been able to let anyone see me, let alone talk to anyone about it and all the problems it creates," said David. There was a note of urgency in David's voice and at that point he would have paid twice as much had she taken advantage of him, but she did not.

Ramona was quite sympathetic, but wary enough to suggest that initially they should just meet somewhere to have a coffee. Then if they felt comfortable with each other, an appointment could be made and she could help him in a more practical way.

The following morning David walked into the Bun Club Cafe, a quite respectable West End coffee establishment favoured by the likes of Ramona. She explained that she would be wearing a black leather ladies' jacket with a brightly-flowered print blouse which stood out in any crowd. He spotted her sitting by herself in a corner reading the morning newspaper.

He walked over. She was wearing sunglasses but other than that effort to hide the eyes he could plainly see she was quite an attractive brunette.

"Ramona, I presume?" David enquired.

"Indeed, I am," replied Ramona as she held out a well-manicured hand. "Please sit down."

David felt a little awkward given the reason why they were meeting. Ramona's voice was that of quite a cultivated woman and her appearance was far from that of a common prostitute. She detected in him a very wound-up tense person, probably going through some agonies of denial as he tried to contain his problem. She came to the point.

"What's the problem, David?"

"Like I tried to explain to you last night, I believe I'm transsexual, completely confused and desperately unhappy. I'm caught in a trap and sometimes I just don't know which way to turn."

"I can sympathize. I was once like that. I was married to a nice woman with whom I had a daughter. I had a promising career with one of the big banks. But in those days human rights laws offered no protection. After I told them of my predicament they fired me."

"Your ad mentioned that you're post-op. Has it been successful?" asked David.

"In physical terms, yes; in terms of settling the serpent in my belly, so to speak, yes; in family terms, no. It cost me my marriage, most of my family relationships and I haven't seen my growing daughter for more than five years. She was ten when I last saw her, so if I ever see her again she'll be a grown-up young woman and I'll have missed one of the most interesting periods in a parent's life, - helping a child grow up and reaching maturity."

"Where is your daughter living?" asked David.

"After our divorce my ex married an American and moved to Alaska. In no way did she want anything further to do with me. In many ways I can hardly blame her as she wanted a man who enjoyed his manhood rather than a man like me who'd only be happy as a woman. Her second husband is mayor of the town where they live and has a sound business there as an agent for an oil company. My ex forbids my daughter to contact me, but I have a lawyer up there to whom I can send my daughter money. The lawyer notifies my daughter to tell her that a sum of money is awaiting collection by her. I do this twice a year on her birthday and at Christmas. The lawyer gets the girl to sit down and write me a thank you letter. That's the only contact I have with my family, but it gives me hope that once she's reached the age of independence she can come down and visit me. The lawyer has explained to her the legalities of her position and my daughter in turn has told him that she wants to see her "daddy" again, so there's some hope. Here, I'm doing all the talking. What about you, David?"

David seemed to come out of a trance. He had been listening intently to everything that Ramona had been telling him. So much so that it had taken him away from his own world with all his own anxieties and worries. Now an innocent, well-meaning acquaintance had asked him a question and it seemed as if he had felt an earth tremor. Ramona thought he seemed very disturbed. Maybe she could help, maybe not.

Ramona helped him out by saying, "I can tell that you're very upset deep down inside. If you don't wish to talk about it, that's your choice. But, David, it'll do you a world of good to start discussing your problems with someone. You mentioned you think you're transsexual. At least you seem to be able to face that. Would it help if you came over one evening and let me give you a makeover. You can bring whatever clothes you have and I can lend you the rest. If you can see your female self and show her to someone else, it may help you relax and tell me something more about yourself."

David's next question seemed quite mundane after Ramona's little exercise in counselling.

"What will a session cost me?"

"For a makeover and dress-up session, $200 for the evening, to end no later than 11 p.m. I'm sorry I have to make a charge, but I'm a working girl and this is how I pay my way."

"Can I give you a call at say 10 tomorrow morning? It's not that I'm being picayune about things, but I have to figure out my timetable over the next few days."

At first she thought he might have a mean streak in him. But then they shook hands and he left her holding a $50 bill. She was happy to have it and made no protest. After all, she was a working girl.

David had enjoyed the brief interlude with Ramona, but then he reverted to his anxieties once again. What was he, David Rakewood, doing drinking coffee with a prostitute? After all, he was driven by his ideas of membership in his upper-crust society. Something was very wrong, the contrast between his station in life as a leading local industrialist and the life led by Ramona was ridiculous. They were poles apart, but no matter how he reasoned all the circumstances of his life, he found himself increasingly out of tune with the upper-crust set. He had come to loath everything they stood for, but he could not cut himself adrift from them. For some reason he had found some hope of relaxation with Ramona, the first person with whom he had voluntarily discussed his inner secrets.

The next morning David picked up the phone and dialled through to Ramona's number. The same husky "Hullo" replied.

"Ramona, this is David. I've thought it over and a make-over is just what I need. I'll bring my case of clothing as you suggest and leave you to do the rest."

Two nights later David relaxed with a glass of Ramona's white wine. She admired his appearance after she had spent some time working over him.

"Everyone has to have a femme name when they go through an experience like this," said Ramona. "I think you look very good, Dianne. If you decide to go through with a gender change you'll improve a great deal under the influence of hormones."

"I'm sure I will if I can ever summon up the courage to do something more about it."

David slowly unfolded the miseries of his life and how his circumstances had him completely trapped.

"Can I make a comment and a suggestion?" asked Ramona.

"Of course you can," he replied, feeling pleasantly relaxed without being under the influence of alcohol.

"Okay. Y'know if you ever have a problem to do with anything sexual, to do something about it takes a great deal of courage and the certainty that it's going to cost a lot in terms of family, friends, and often your position in life. But Dianne, it's something you have to deal with if you're ever going to have any peace and happiness in life. Living life with severe repression and secrecy is a sure way to have a real crisis to deal with one day. You become like a boiler with too much steam pressure. If it ever blows up, that's the end of you."

Ramona did not know she was forecasting David's future as she continued. "If I were you I'd go to see a psychiatrist. I'm happy to help with makeovers and such, but to be honest it's no long-term answer for the rest of your life."

David did visit Ramona on several more occasions. He also did as she suggested and saw a psychiatrist.

* * * * *

David's visits to the psychiatrist helped, but he could not unburden himself of all his innermost secrets. He did, however, talk about his repressed desire to be of the opposite sex and the fact that this was his greatest regret. The psychiatrist went as far as he could with David and then suggested that as this appeared to be a clear case of deep-seated gender dysphoria he wished to refer him to Dr. Margaret Myers, a noted specialist in this field.

At the first meeting with Dr. Myers, David found it quite difficult to go over all the ground which he had covered with his previous psychiatrist. Gradually she put him at his ease as he came to realize that he was now in the hands of a recognized expert.

"What I find so disturbing about all this, Doctor, is that in reality I have everything that a man could want: a great family and a wife I tell myself I love, a home of which I am very proud and a good business and we enjoy a social position. All of this could blow away like so much sand on the beach if my problems ever came out into the open. My wife, who has been brought up to be socially conscious, would be devastated. Our friends would treat me like a leper. There's no place for misfits in our type of society which worships success and personal wealth. Our children, who are at private schools, would be shunned by their class-mates. The possibilities are endless, but yet I know that something has to be done about it all before I go mad. Now, I find myself making friends with a prostitute, but at present she's the only true friend I have. I don't want to sound like a snob because that's not my intention, but it surely must be a matter of going from the sublime to the ridiculous."

Dr. Myers mostly listened on this first meeting. She could see that David's condition was made all the more complex by his social perceptions which may or may not be well-founded. She noticed his statement, "I have a wife I tell myself I love." Why did he have to use such a term? Surely he either loved her or he didn't. But at least his own assessment of the type of society in which he and his wife prospered was probably pretty accurate. To what extent he suffered from an overblown ego and how heavily was his life based on false values and empty pride was too early to say.

"I don't see anything too wrong with making friends with a prostitute. It sounds as though she has all the understanding and compassion that your social set is lacking. You say she is a former transsexual. At least she's showing you the way with the benefit of some experience. She's also showing you what you might fall into if you go ahead with a gender change. This might particularly apply if your every move is not well thought out."

His reference to his wife's socially conscious view of their lives spelled trouble in handling any positive moves David might make to ease his condition. Between this meeting and the next Dr. Myers made some subtle enquiries to develop a better picture of David and Kathy's family backgrounds.

When next they met about two weeks later, Dr. Myers commenced the interview by making it clear that she had a better background on many aspects of David's life. He was content to assume that she had been piecing together whatever she needed to develop this background.

"I can see, Mr. Rakewood, why your concerns are so strong about family reactions and how destructive any leakage of your problem could be to everything you hold dear to you. Just how we can help you in that regard is very hard to predict. Unfortunately, the nature of gender dysphoria is that just as you had no choice in the selection processes of nature and have had to suffer its consequences silently and in private, so also are there certain things which you have to face alone. We can explain and add credibility to it all, but in the final analysis you are the one who has to face the music. I am more than willing to meet your wife in the near future, but I can't work miracles if she has her mind set like concrete. By your explanation of her values I do foresee problems," concluded Dr. Myers.

David had agreed to think about this and to see Dr. Myers again in three weeks' time. Silently he had resolved to broach the subject to his wife. He knew that there were inherent dangers which depended so much on her reaction and he would need time to think it all out. One thing of which he was now convinced was that he could not put off this vital move for very much longer. His consumption of alcohol was increasing dramatically, which was really a symptom of running away from his inner problem. But he did notice that when he was dressed up at Ramona's his need for alcohol largely disappeared. Instead of downing a half bottle of scotch in the evening, a glass of Ramona's white wine would last all evening and if she offered tea he would drink it. He supposed that because he was enjoying a little contentment, this explained his virtual rejection of alcohol. To him there were almost as many dangers in heavy dependence on alcohol as there were in connection with his gender dysphoric condition. David truly saw himself as being caught between a rock and a hard place.

* * * * *

In plain English, Kathy Rakewood would rank as a bitch of the first magnitude to many, even in her own circle. It was not for nothing that behind her back she was known as the Ice Queen, cold, beautiful, calculating and possessed by her need to be the leading glamorous establishment wife who in her decorous way was invariably at the centre of the social whirl.

She did not know or care how others viewed her. David played it down and tried to ignore it. His feeling towards his wife, if no longer one of passionate love, was one by which he treated her with civility and respect. He hung onto an old-fashioned concept of loyalty to his wife, come what may. At first Kathy appreciated this in the early days of their marriage, but eventually she became tired of it as the years passed. David bored her, there was no excitement, sex such as it was, was a featureless duty that followed the same old routine. But above all Kathy could not permit the thought to enter her mind that for some reason she might be to blame for much of this state of affairs.

Instead, there were far younger, more virile and infinitely more handsome men that Kathy could have any time she wanted. A lunch at an upscale hotel, with Tom, Dick or Harry invariably became an afternoon of passionate love making in her hotel room during the afternoon, which might well turn into an evening event.

On this occasion Kathy was visiting her hair, nails and lashes studio. Her incredible beauty notwithstanding, always required embellishment in her view of herself. Carlo, a handsome but somewhat effeminate Italian was the owner and her own special hairdresser. Her type wanted only the best of several treatments offered at Carlo's. A hair colouring, restyling, a set, manicure and pedicure were all indulged in and, now and again she had her lashes attended to. It was only after all these gratifications that Kathy could see herself as being beautiful. As she sat there awaiting the next stage in her beauty treatment, she examined her long slender nails from which the varnish had been removed, the cuticles pushed back and the nails prepared for a fresh replenishment of several coats of nail polish. She would not be happy with her nails until they shone like jewels at the ends of her fingers.

Carlo was mincing around and possessed the happy facility of drawing his customers out and this particular morning was no exception. Last night, David had told Kathy of the full extent of his misery through his gender dysphoria condition. This time she held her tongue while he recounted everything of his inner feelings and frustrations. Her quietness as she listened beguiled him into thinking that he might be getting through to her and just maybe she was showing some willingness to understand. This time it was also a different David speaking as he quietly spoke from the bottom of his heart. She did not interrupt, but on occasion allowed a smile to cross her face following some remark and at last David came to the end of his explanation with the words "so there it is. I've told you everything that I can think of."

As he relaxed in his chair he leaned back hoping and half expecting an intelligent response that might at last show some understanding of his gender identity challenges. Kathy smiled sardonically to herself as she thought of her response of last night.

"Okay, you've said your piece and I think it's all bullshit." David's hands went to his face as if he had been struck a mortal blow and in a sense he received just that.

"Oh, my God!. What have I done?" His voice expressed his horror as his anxiety level shot up like a runaway thermometer.

"What you've done with your own lips has been to destroy our marriage. That's what you've done." The words ripped out of Kathy dripping with venom. "First, if you have known all your life that you have a problem with internalized gender dysphoria, you should never have married me. You married under false pretences. You should have gone down to the West End and found yourself some boy friends. There's lots down there like you."

"But I'm not gay. I've already explained all that." A note of resentment was detectable in David's voice.

"Another thing. You had no right to father my children. What if you have infected them with your problems. You might even have had a bearing on little Jimmy's death." Kathy was running all this through her mind, as she thought maybe she had been too hard on David. Just the same she made a mental note to seek the advice of a divorce lawyer. She was musing like this when Carlo returned. Almost involuntarily she spoke out, knowing full well that Carlo was gay.

"Carlo, what do you do about a husband who wants to be a woman?"

"Send him down here and we'll give him a complete makeover. By the time we've finished he won't know himself." Carlo smiled at his own humour.

"No don't try to be funny, Carlo. I'm serious. You make no bones about being gay and I respect you for your honesty. But suddenly my husband has come out with the statement that he's a transsexual and I don't know how to handle it. It's come as a complete surprise. I've read about them in the papers and it all sounds pretty disgusting," said Kathy.

Carlo turned serious for a change and in quiet measured words explained a few things to Kathy. "Mrs. Rakewood, if he is transsexual you can be sure he's almost certainly telling the truth and there is no pill he can take to get rid of it, because it's a life long condition. You're born with it and you die with it. I've met a few in gay bars, but they are not usually gays."

"Why do they go there then?" Kathy asked slightly puzzled.

"Because they often feel more secure with gays. The gays usually won't try to come onto them or get aggressive. Gays more easily adopt a live and let live attitude." Carlo paused for a moment while Kathy knitted her eye-brows. Carlo could see she was puzzled as he made a gesture in the direction of one of his clients.

"Do you see that nice looking older lady at the end station?"

"Yes, I can see her in the mirror."

"She's a transsexual who had surgery a good many years ago. She was a professional man. Some sort of accountant who stayed in her job until retirement. Her firm in which she was a partner didn't throw her out. She's a very nice lady, very considerate and all she expects from us is courtesy and good service in return. We know her background but it never enters the picture. She's a respected customer and we treat her that way. She still lives with her former wife, who also comes in here and they're the best of friends," responded Carlo. "She's not a male gay in drag, she may now define as being lesbian, but she's a responsible, decent citizen and that's how it is with many transsexuals. I didn't say all, but I do mean many of them and I say that from first hand experience."

"Why are you telling me all this Carlo?" Kathy sounded almost as though she was suspicious of a con job.

"No reason, other than to let you know that I appreciate your anxieties, but also to let you know that in this day and age it is no big deal. It can be handled sensibly or destructively. It can be dealt with comfortably or there can be a lot of agony to spread around. It's as simple as that."

Kathy changed the subject. This was not what she wanted to hear. It was all too reasonable and real people could not be expected to handle it so simply. The session was over.

"Please treat what I've told you as a secret, Carlo. It would not do if it became the subject of gossip."

"You can rely on me, Mrs. Rakewood. I hear all sorts of secrets but I keep them to myself."

* * * * *

Last night David could see that Kathy was quite paranoid and liable to became even more irrational as she flew off the handle. He quietly got up, walked to the wine cabinet, poured a stiff scotch, went out to his car and drove over to his sister Elizabeth Sadler's place. He did not break down. He was in shock and just felt the need for some human company and a secure place where he could recover his composure. He didn't tell the Sadlers about the subject of the argument with Kathy, dismissing it all with a remark that "we had another fight." The pity of it was that had he taken his sister and brother-in-law into his confidence it might have been the first step on his road to a satisfactory outcome for his problems.

A week later David reviewed all these circumstances and memories in his mind as he sat there in his car. His last interview with Dr. Myers had taken place two months previously and now his memories brought him to his current position, severely depressed and deeply troubled. Dr. Myers had done whatever she could, but she was up against the impenetrable wall of Kathy's resistance and David's self-defence mechanism by which he could not forget his social status. Kathy's attitude towards psychiatrists was at best most unflattering. The two had met just once and in spite of the doctor's patient attempt at explanation, Kathy would make allowance for nothing, not weakening at all in her position of total denial.

Kathy had made no bones about it all. She wanted David out and would only allow him to return when he was able to convince her that he had put all this transsexual nonsense out of his mind and was ready to resume a normal life. The alternative was a divorce with all its complex ramifications. He shuddered to think in his imagination of what people would say if all this leaked out. He ran the labels through his mind: shallow, selfish, queer, gay, pervert, monster. Each took on a greater intensity as the fleeting glimpses of his family, his friends and many business connections passed in steady array through his tortured mind like apparitions before him, accusing, mocking, sneering, making ignorant sarcastic comments, commiserating with Kathy on whom they would layer their sympathies.

The spectre of all this was too overpowering. David knew their thought processes well enough. He knew how he would probably think if some other poor soul was the affected one and he was in the position of being the judge. It never occurred to him that there might actually be those among "the crowd" who might have judged him less severely, who might have had some compassion, who tempered their judgements with humanity and sympathy, who might have some understanding or at least shown some willingness to learn. What about his sisters, Helen and Elizabeth? To Elizabeth as the youngest sibling in his family he was a hero. She was always warm and friendly toward her brother and probably would have been his best confidante. How could he tell? After all, he never discussed his problem with anyone, least of all his sister. Had he done so he might have been agreeably surprised. Everyone was not like Kathy – thank God!.

As he pictured his friends he saw them all as a bunch of hungry carnivores, fangs bared like jackals ready for the kill. The thought made him shudder as he thought of a simpler, kinder life among ordinary people who lacked the pretensions of his social set. Somehow reaching out and finding a comfortable place in such a society seemed to him to be like a mirage.

In his frightened mind his peers would ask how in hell Kathy ever got together with a freak like David? They would wonder how he came to be infected with it, was it passed down from his father and his grandfather before him and would his children catch the same bug?

Added to this was his inability to shake off the shackles of his own social values, after all, people in his position just did not get involved in such scandalous behaviour. He took a flask out of his glove compartment and drained the contents. The warming effect of the Scotch whisky, added to his earlier consumption, gave him Dutch courage. Now he made up his mind to end it all. He switched on the ignition, reversed out of the empty parking lot and then changing gear into forward slowly drove up the road for about a mile to a mail box.

He got out and walked unsteadily across the road to the box and dropped several letters inside. The car radio was blaring out a raucous cacophony of riotous rock music, the sound seeming to grate on the respectable silence which pervaded the area. It was 3 a.m. on that fateful Sunday morning and no one was around at this hour. Somehow early Sunday mornings when the mists hung low and soft rain came down always seemed to be the scene for his depression ridden ramblings. He did a U-turn and then booted the accelerator as hard as he could. The tires screamed and gave off blue smoke as the powerful motor roared like a jet engine at take-off. The car increased speed from about 30 to 60 to around 120 km/h and still climbing. The parking lot was at a turn in the road as he raced through it and hit the stoutly-built wooden barrier which shattered into a thousand fragments. The car bounced across the ornamental rockery and flew into the air as it went over the cliff and fell several hundred feet to the rocks below landing on its roof, breaking David's neck, as the steering wheel came back into his chest, then bouncing over and over before coming to a dead stop.

There was a smell of gasoline and suddenly the entire neighbourhood was illuminated by an explosion of burning gas. David's misery was over as he was cremated in the wreck of his car.......

Chapter Three

The Mystery Fire

The wild drive along the road and the car which became a projectile when it penetrated the barrier and flew like a demented hornet over the cliff, was not witnessed by anyone. Not so the explosion and fire which followed when the vehicle came to rest. The lightkeeper at the lighthouse across the bay had seen the giant flare caused by the explosion and straightaway felt that a boat had blown up. He called Air-Sea Rescue and soon a helicopter was airborne with a floodlight for night time examinations. A tugboat, which was closer to the fire, also talked to Air-Sea Rescue and then called the city police as they were close enough to be uncertain as to whether it was another boat close inshore or a land-based fire.

The mate of the tugboat *Salish Prince* was on watch and simultaneously pressed a buzzer to the skipper's cabin to alert him to the possibility of an emergency. As the skipper entered the wheelhouse he exclaimed, "Holy God, what an inferno!" as he told the mate to slow down and circle with their barge so that they could see what was going on.

"What do you think it is, Bob, a boat, a plane that has crashed along the shore or something on fire on the beach?" asked the skipper addressing the mate.

"Holy Mother of suffering Christ! I can't tell for certain. There wuzz a huge explosion and then it giv' off a mushroom sorta cloud and then it died down some. I think it's up on the beach if these glasses are tellin' no lies. Luk, there's a police car and in the distance I see the lights of more emergency vehicles," Bob said handing the binoculars to the skipper.

By now they had lowered a wheelhouse window and opened the door to the bridge deck outside. The wailing of several sirens could be heard as vehicles raced to the site of the fire.

"I guess we'd better get back on course. There's nuthin' we can do. It's on shore and now there's lotsa help on the way," said the skipper.

By the time the police and a fire engine had arrived there was nothing left to do. The fire-fighters could see that from the height they were at they could pump water in a fine spray so that it would envelope the now smoldering car and cool the wreck down. That way the two police officers could get near to it. The remains of a very badly charred body could be seen behind the wheel which had been crushed back into the driver's chest just as the roof had come down on his head.

As the wreck could not be retrieved from above, a barge was brought into the beach later that day and the remains were winched on board and then removed to the police yard. A forensic expert's report stated, "Assuming it was the remains of a man, he probably died when the car first landed on its fore end. The wheel was pushed back and crushed his chest and then rolled over onto its roof, which then broke his neck. Seconds later gasoline exploded and the flames engulfed the vehicle cremating the body."

Any identification was impossible except for the burned license and registration plates which were removed by the police. On checking ownership the car was found to be a leased vehicle and the leasing company quickly confirmed that its contract was with Rakewood Fabricators Limited, the designated driver being David Rakewood.

An interview with Mrs. Kathy Rakewood revealed that her husband had moved out, was drinking heavily and had been receiving psychiatric counselling from Dr. Margaret Myers whom she had met just the once.

A woman detective visited Dr. Myers at her clinic. She raised the privacy issue and wanted undertakings from the police that the sensitive information she was going to give in a client/physician relationship was not to be released to the press.

"We understand where you're coming from Doctor. What you tell us is for use in our investigation and not for publication. But you do understand, I hope, that there will be a coroner's enquiry and you will obviously be called to testify under oath. Matters will then move into the public domain regardless and because Mr. Rakewood was a prominent figure in the business world there'll be lots of attention from the media," said the policewoman conducting the interview.

"Okay, I understand that. But for the moment my main concern is to shield the family from idle tongues and speculation. I realize that when it gets into the coroner's office the file will be as complete as it can be for the enquiry and then it will all come out." Dr. Myers felt badly for the family and was relieved to have the police undertaking as she gave her account of her consultations with David Rakewood.

"David Rakewood was gender dysphoric, or transsexual if you prefer, meaning that he suffered from a biological abnormality which gave rise to his gender identity disorder. That in turn was the root of a powerful deep-seated urge to be a member of his opposite sex. It is a condition which most people have extreme difficulty understanding and many reject outright. From a psychiatrist's point of view it is not too hard to successfully treat, although this fairly commonly will involve a sex change, which is often the sufferer's deepest desire. Mr. Rakewood's case was made very difficult for him to handle for social reasons and because his wife was unable to understand and did not wish to understand, anything of his predicament. Her attitude increased his agony and made him feel entirely alone when he most needed a soul mate in whom he could confide. Instead, all he could see was someone, himself, who was thoroughly condemned in his own mind."

The detective was puzzled by what the doctor told her. "I can see how his anxiety led to his final crisis when he apparently took his own life. I suppose it's quite typical of many situations when a person is driven to despair for whatever reason. Of course, I know a little of transsexualism, but I had no idea it could have this effect on a wealthy man who seems to have had everything," said the detective.

"That's the conventional view, but it can hit at any level of society, young or old, male or female," replied Dr. Myers.

"Yes, I suppose that's so. We come across transsexuals on the street, people who have nothing and little hope of ever improving themselves, sometimes HIV-infected and often committed to drugs or alcohol or both. They have no future, few can help them and no one wants them."

"Of course," said Dr. Myers, "but you only hear of the ones who make the police blotter and the public only those who hit the headlines, often for some silly reason. The media needs a story and the public, with its insatiable fascination with anything it sees as being sex with a difference, laps it all up like a kitten drinks its milk. I can tell you that this practice has treated a fair number of gender dysphoria cases and we always have some active files making their way through the process of change and they come from all walks in life. Most manage to handle it with discretion and it does become a whole lot easier all around if the patient has a supportive family. Regrettably a great many don't and Mr. Rakewood, who had everything else, never had that, at least so far as Mrs. Rakewood was concerned."

After talking generally about the medical aspects of the condition and the fact that Mr. Rakewood had not reached the stage of taking hormones, the policewoman moved to take her leave.

"Thank you, Dr. Myers. We now have positive identification and we've found a diary in his locked desk drawer which more or less agrees with what you have said. There will be a coroner's enquiry to which you will be required to attend as a professional expert witness. Oh, I almost forgot. Does the name 'Ramona' mean anything to you?" the detective asked.

"Only that David Rakewood had mentioned that he had come to know her. She assisted him in make-up and dressing lessons. That's something with which many transsexuals need help. She's a call girl and advertises her special services in the local gay/lesbian paper. I don't think there was any matter of sexual relief, but you should have no difficulty in finding her if you look in the classified ads" replied Dr. Myers.

The following day Dr. Myers received one of the letters which David had posted just before his suicide ride in his car. She read it with care and saw a writer who was in a deeply depressed, thoroughly upset and totally negative frame of mind. Attached were copies of letters he had sent to his wife and the two children. In them David asked for forgiveness and understanding, at the same time as he blamed his predicament less on the fact that he suffered from gender dysphoria and more on the unforgiving nature of the society which surrounded him. In the letter he wrote to Dr. Myers, he asked that the entire file be turned over to the coroner as he felt it important that the full story should come out and not just some garbled version. Clearly he did not expect his own wife to make them available to the coroner.

At the inquest, Dr. Myers described in detail her attendance on her patient to a sympathetic coroner. A surprise followed when the coroner called Sylvia Leighton to the stand. The court clerk asked her to take the Bible and give the customary oath.

"Ms. Leighton, you are in business under the name Ramona. Do you agree?"

"Yes," she replied.

"What is your business?"

"I provide services to lonely gentlemen for a fee."

"Thank you, Ms. Leighton. Can you describe the services you provided to the deceased, David Rakewood?"

"Mr. Rakewood called me in response to my ad in the local underground newspaper. You see, I'm also a transsexual and readily admit it. He wanted assistance in learning about make-up and proper feminine dressing."

"Why do you think he chose you instead of the several others who advertise?"

"Because, I'd stated in my ad that I'm transsexual."

"Please give me your general impression of his problems as he relayed them to you," asked the coroner.

"I think his biggest problem was severe loneliness. He'd no one to talk to who'd had any understanding of his problem. He needed a kindred soul and I guess I might'ave been the most obvious. It wouldn't have been the first time I've been contacted by someone similarly troubled. He told me quite a lot about his home and social life and it wasn't encouraging for a person trying to deal with a gender problem. I think more than anything else he was frightened of rejection from his own family and his peer group. I urged him to get psychiatric help."

"Did he strike you as being suicidal?" asked the coroner.

"Not at the time, although he was suffering great anxiety and was obviously under a lot of personal pressure. When he was cross-dressed he seemed like a far different person, quite happy and, by comparison, relatively carefree and relaxed. He did not want any sexual favours and didn't drink anything beyond a glass of white wine."

"How many glasses did he have when he visited?

"Usually just one, but never more than two," replied Ms. Leighton.

"When was the last time he visited you?"

Ramona consulted her diary. "On April 25th, about two months ago."

"Thank you Ms. Leighton. You may step down," said the coroner.

Needless to say Kathy Rakewood was present and was also called as the wife of the deceased. She attempted to cloak the whole affair, professing that her knowledge of what had been the probable root cause was limited to the one meeting she had with Dr. Myers. She was clearly embarrassed by what came out at the hearing and doubly embarrassed the following day when the results of the hearing were reported in the local newspapers.

She was badly shaken when the coroner asked her if she had received any communication from her husband in the form of a letter posted just before his death. She admitted that she had, but agreed that she had not turned it over to the inquest as she considered it private business limited to her and her alone.

The coroner held up the copy letters provided by Dr. Myers. "I have copies of the letters your husband wrote to you and your two children, but I don't propose to read them to the inquest. This is the kind of highly personal writing which doesn't need to be turned into a public spectacle."

The coroner added, "But these are the simple words of a man giving up on life. It is interesting to note that he blamed no one specifically for his predicament, but in asking for forgiveness in taking his own life he made it clear that there was much room for a far more sympathetic and intelligent response from society generally. He evidently developed a low opinion of his social group whom he referred to as a 'modern-day Cliveden set,' a social group who I understand was very close to the monarchy in England at one time. From what little I know of their history they sort of set the standards of social acceptability and social excess in their time."

Kathy had been indirectly admonished by the coroner when he remarked on how quickly couples forget their marriage vows when they pledge to look after their spouses through sickness and adversity, but at the first sign of serious trouble leave the sufferer to suffer alone with all his or her shame, much of it self-inflicted.

"It's a very selective process, it seems," continued the coroner. If a spouse had cancer or toothache, a broken leg or a torn ligament all of these maladies would have been respectable and therefore acceptable to spouses, families and others. They are dealt with in the ordinary course of living or dying.

"The root of Mr. Rakewood's problem was his gender dysphoria, a condition which, expert opinion tells us, afflicts certain of us humans in the formative stage when we are a fetus in our mother's womb. If the condition is there it is unavoidable and it's as basic to the sufferer as the colour of the skin or eyes. Precisely what happens hasn't been seen by the human eye and may in fact never be seen. The story of Mr. Rakewood's life included his continuous battle to control the condition and the instinctive force it releases.

"The illness which brought about his death while biological in origin, was psychological and the stresses and anxieties that it threw off caused him in all likelihood to turn to alcohol as a way of getting away from his problems. There is no evidence of drugs although in this era drugs is the more common choice as a means of hiding away from the effects of the dysphoria. The gender dysphoria was the primary cause of his discomfort with life and the alcohol was what ate away at his life and destroyed the roots upon which his health depended. A more easily understood colloquialism might well be that he died of a broken heart. Wiser handling by those closest to him and development of a capability on his part to adjust his societal values would have brought about a better end result in every likelihood. It was hardly surprising that he sought companionship outside of the marriage. It's a good thing that Ms. Leighton was available when needed. In fact it was on her good advice that he saw a psychiatrist in an effort to gain some professional help."

The verdict returned by the coroner was "that the deceased took his own life while the balance of his mind was disturbed."

* * * * *

As Kathy left the coroner's office following the hearing she was suddenly confronted by an unpleasant fact of life to which she had given scant regard. A couple of reporters and photographers were standing just outside the entrance.

She was accompanied by her lawyer, Simon Guthrie. As the reporters sidled up to Kathy the usual questions were shot out.

"How come you had no idea that this might happen with your late husband, Mrs. Rakewood?"

Mr. Guthrie, who was also a family friend and secretary of Rakewood Fabricators, muttered, "Look straight ahead and ignore them, Kathy. You don't have to say a word you don't want to."

"How are the kids handling it?"

"What are your plans, Mrs. Rakewood?" came further questions.

Guthrie reached his car and opened the door for Kathy. As soon as he had closed it he turned on the reporters. "Have you guys got no bloody compassion? The lady has just been put over the rack and has had quite enough for one day. Anyhow, let's forget this 'freedom of the press and the public has the right to know' bullshit. She's not talking to you now, tomorrow or ever on a tragic private family matter. So back off guys."

By now he had taken up his own position at the wheel of his Jaguar. "You'll get this for a few days, Kathy. I expect there'll be others standing on the pavement outside your house who'll try to waylay us. We'll ignore them. If you get phone calls say nothing once you've identified the party and simply hang up. If they persist take the handpiece off and if it goes on ask the phone company for an unlisted number. Eventually they'll get tired of it."

Until now Kathy had said almost nothing. "What sort of ghouls are these people that they can't leave a family alone in their misery?"

"I agree, but there are people who revel in someone's else's misery if they feel it'll make news and news means money for these sharks. You'll just have to harden your heart. If I know the way these things go, the next lot will be television people, followed by people wanting stories for the supermarket tabloids. Don't be surprised if someone even offers you money for your exclusive story. Just remember you're under no obligation to anyone and if it gets beyond the nuisance type like today tell them to get in touch with me."

By now they were a minute off the entrance to the driveway to the Rakewood home, a show place set in large parklike grounds with many trees and banks of shrubs. Sure enough the reporters were gathered in a bunch on the pavement. "We can't do anything about that unless they block access or actually go on the grounds." Guthrie drove at a slow safe speed through the reporters who were forced to make way. When he was about 30 metres in he stopped the car and wound down the window, having spotted two photographers walking on the lawn. "Get out immediately. I'm calling the police and I'll have you arrested for trespass."

"God, this is really too much," Kathy said through her tears. "What am I going to do if this sort of harassment goes on."

"Look, Kathy. You're going to get it just like I said. Why don't you pack a few things and come and stay with Millicent and me for a few days? Plan a holiday after you've made arrangements with the kids."

Simon Guthrie was doing his level best to provide the support and protection he knew Kathy needed as she was now at her most vulnerable. Privately, he had a lot of sympathy for David who had been his friend and golfing partner on many occasions, although he had no idea that David had also been a secret transsexual. He knew a fair amount about the subject as he had once defended a transsexual in a murder case and managed to obtain a manslaughter verdict. If only David had been able to talk about his problems with someone like himself there might have been a better outcome. He also felt sympathy for Kathy but knew she had the sort of personality that created problems for herself and others with whom she came into contact, including David's youngest sister Elizabeth.

* * * * *

Elaine and Alan Rakewood were devastated by the death of their father but in differing ways. Alan was about 16 when the tragedy happened and in an exclusive boys' school. The word quickly got around as other boys attending the school had parents who knew Alan's parents. No one knew quite what to say or how to handle the situation. The Simpson boys were probably the closest and tried to sympathize with Alan who clearly did not want to discuss his father's death with anyone. Brian Simpson who was the older of the two brothers spoke to the assistant head master and told him all he knew about the Rakewood family. Mr. Royle, the master suggested that Alan should stay home for a few days. However, Alan couldn't tell Mr. Royle why he didn't want to be in the same home as his mother at this time, but her attitude had always made him feel uncomfortable.

"Do you have any other relative with whom you could perhaps stay. You are 16 and you do have a choice in the matter," advised Mr. Royle.

"Yes, there's my aunt, Mrs. Sadler who lives not far away. I could ask her. There may be complications though," replied the boy.

"Oh! How do you mean?"

"Mother and Mrs. Sadler don't like each other, but she was my father's sister and I like her and her husband."

"Why don't you ask her? Then we'll let your mother know, as we are obliged to," suggested Mr. Royle.

Alan phoned his aunt and uncle from the school. Elizabeth answered, "Yes, of course you can stay with us, but you'll have to let your mother know."

It was just before the inquest and Kathy Rakewood seemed to her son to be in a daze.

Alan knew his mother would be enraged when he spoke to her, so her reply when it came surprised him. She sounded almost relieved when she said "Yes, you may if that's okay with your aunt and uncle."

For Kathy it was a different story when she received a collect phone call from Elaine a few days after the news of her father's death filtered through to her at her hippie commune on the West Coast of Vancouver Island.

"Mom, it's Elaine. I'm calling from a pay phone near the beach at Tofino. It's very windy and I can hardly hear you."

Kathy raised her voice. "You've heard of Dad's death, I guess."

"Yes, I have and I'm heart-broken. I found it in one of the Vancouver papers in a local coffeeshop. I'm coming home as soon as I can catch the next bus."

"Okay, I understand," replied Kathy.

"You understand you say. It's a pity you never understood Dad. If you had he might have still been alive. You were his wife and partner, but when he needed help from you it just was never there."

"That's enough Elaine. We'll discuss all this when you come home."

Kathy had a sense of foreboding. First her son didn't want to stay at home and now her daughter was coming home with blood in her eye. When and where would all this end?

The next day, Elaine arrived carrying her guitar under one arm and her other belongings in a large knapsack on her back. Her Indian wool jacket was wet with rainwater and matched the toque she wore on her head. To complete the ensemble she was wearing loggers type caulk boots. She anticipated a poor reception when she came to the family home so she went to the rear of the house to make her entrance.

As soon as Kathy saw her daughter her hands went to her face. "Oh, my God, what a mess" was her reaction.

"Jesus, Mom, save the mock horror. Yes, it's me, your daughter Elaine and believe me you can't camp on a beach, wearin' a crinoline, on the West Coast of Vancouver Island, when it's pissin' with rain and the wind is blowin' at a 100K."

For a moment Kathy was lost for words as Elaine dumped all her gear on the floor and pulled her boots off. "I need a damned good bath. In fact I'd like to soak for an hour. Do I still have a bed here and I hope some of my clothes are still hanging up in the closet."

"Yes, everything thing is still there as you left it a year ago. Have your bath and then we'll talk."

* * * * *

A few days later Kathy Rakewood came into Dr. Myers' office in a more contrite mood and was willing to listen. Of course by now the opportunity for any other result in David's life had been lost. Dr. Myers had anticipated this meeting with some trepidation. She was normally a very compassionate and relaxed person. At their first meeting she had found Kathy Rakewood to be overbearing and arrogant and the coroner's hearing had done nothing to dispel this.

"The problem was not helped by your attitude, Mrs. Rakewood. I'm not suggesting that you were responsible for his suicide as there were other factors, such as his concern about condemnation within his and your family quite apart from your social circle.

"You know, if people would just try to understand by listening and talking and allowing the affected person to unburden himself of his stresses and anxieties this type of tragedy would be more avoidable. Instead what happens too frequently is that, pumped full of their own prejudices and ignorance, they talk to a lawyer first, before even thinking of listening to a psychiatrist. In any event, we can only do so much.

"If goodwill and any desire to help or understand is lacking," continued Dr. Myers, "Total rejection follows and the sufferer, like your David, feels as bad or maybe worse than a person condemned to a leper's colony. His state of mind had convinced him that he had lost you, your children and his home without hope of redemption. I think he saw it all rather like a man on death row awaiting his certain end and having run out of all hopes of reprieve. Your husband had considerable prestige in the business community and the prospect of having to deal with all his business friends heightened his agony."

Kathy's strained expression betrayed her fears and feelings, but at least she could now see the matter from a different and better perspective. "I realize how wrongly I handled this thing from the beginning, and how badly bound I am by false values. I spend too much time concerning myself about how other people, particularly our friends and families, would react to all this. Friends have phoned me to commiserate and to blame David, but even though our children and myself are swept up in this tragedy and spilled milk cannot be recovered, I've urged them not to blame David. He was also the victim of my own and our circle's actual or anticipated condemnation. It behooves us not to condemn him now as we shouldn't have done when he was alive.

"Believe me, Doctor, I've learned a lot after the stable door has been left open and the horse has bolted. David's life could've been saved with a little more charity and an effort to understand. Certainly there would have been a lot of adjustments. Had he gone the way, I recognize now, that he should have, we obviously couldn't have remained man and wife, but we could at least have remained good friends, if only for the sake of our children. I can only hope that, now that his tortured spirit has been released it'll find some happiness wherever he is. If you could see his state of mind when you mention death row, couldn't you have given us some forewarning?"

Dr. Myers let Mrs. Rakewood have her full say. She was obviously going through a period of regret and self-criticism. What a pity, she thought, that people first have to destroy before they can rebuild. She felt sure that over time David Rakewood would have responded quite fully to treatment if only his wife had let him. Given time, problems could have been worked out and a far happier conclusion would have had a chance.

Dr. Myers drew a deep breath and chose her words with great care. "What you've said by way of regret was acceptable and appropriate until you came to your last sentence when you suggested I should have given you some forewarning. You suggest that I as a consulting psychiatrist, was in some way remiss in not taking you by the hair and dragging you kicking and screaming into a scene which, prior to your late husband's death, you simply did not want to know about. Resentment and anger were your emotional responses, not love or compassion. When we first met you reacted in much the same way as you would to a snake oil doctor trying to sell some sort of universal cure-all. Normally, we would all react with scepticism to that kind of situation. But in this instance you not only failed to get with it, even worse, you did all you could to deny its existence as being anything other than an aberration which David would have to get over somehow by himself. Above all, you denied with every morsel of your being that David even had a right to be transsexual. In other words you were in denial, a factor about as useless as suggesting that cancer did not exist in a cancer patient when he might have been expiring before your eyes.

"That's not my idea of fair reciprocity in a relationship, where both parties claim to love each other," added Dr. Myers. More than that, it creates a very sterile background for a psychiatrist to try to help David put the pieces of his life back together again. We psychiatrists can only do so much. With your attitude, combined with the false and shallow social values which you both suffered from, he came up against a stone wall and, frankly sooner or later so would we."

Kathy was crying now. Margaret Myers thought to herself: 'Go ahead, Honey, it'll do you good. At least it shows that you have some sort of emotional response, even though it's in the wrong direction and too late.'

Kathy composed herself and braced her shoulders as she said between sobs. "I didn't like hearing what you said, Doctor, but for the first time in my life someone has at last spoken the naked truth. You're right and I can see I was very wrong. I hope I'll have more compassion with the next troubled person who crosses my path."

"That's good advice you've given yourself, Mrs. Rakewood. Should you be asking for my advice I would strongly urge you to try and undo some of the damage I suspect this sad event has done to your children. Remember that David was their father who, in spite of everything, tried to do his best for his family. He never deserted his family. Because you didn't want him around, you effectively threw him out. Now I think the challenge for you is going to be to admit to your children that their father was not a bad man after all and that he should not have been condemned before, now or later. The psychological damage of all this could take years to work its way to the surface and its possible effects should be allowed for."

Kathy and the doctor shook hands as they parted company. Dr. Myers wondered if Mrs. Rakewood had really learned from her experience. Only time would tell.

* * * * *

Kathy was not looking forward to going home to two children who she felt, rightly enough, were hostile to her. She felt she had righted one upset connection following her meeting with Dr. Myers. Even though she had proclaimed her good intentions when she met 'the next troubled person who crossed her path,' as she had aptly described her feelings of the moment, her own good advice to herself was quickly forgotten when she met her children again that very day.

Alan had returned from several days of living with David's sister, Elizabeth Sadler and her stockbroker husband, but the boy was morose and sullen and clearly had no wish to discuss his father's death or his own hopes for his future. He had actually enjoyed living with the Sadlers, seeing them and their children as being a real family, and he had not failed to notice the manner in which his own mother seemed to go out of her way to snub the Sadlers. He noticed for instance that they had been relegated to a secondary seat in the burial ceremony while his father's coffin stood before the alter of the church near where he and his mother and sister sat. He wondered why the Sadlers were not seated in a front pew or at least only one behind them as after all Aunt Elizabeth was his father's sister and someone of whom David had been very fond.

Kathy arrived home with an inner feeling of apprehension which she tried in hide from her children behind her usual facade of arrogance. Elaine was the first to puncture it however, when she asked her mother how the interview with her father's psychiatrist had gone.

"Oh, fine, fine, thank you" replied Kathy as airily as she could.

"Mother, get with it. You know it was anything but fine. Do you think we're blind or something? First, the press reports were not kind to you and second, I got hold of the transcript of the coroner's hearing, seeing as you forbade either of us to attend," asked Elaine who was obviously short on patience, but it was enough to stir up her mother's anger.

"How the hell did you get hold of that?" was the immediate response from Kathy.

"That's my business and I'm not about to tell you. Just remember this; I'm no longer a child. I could have gone to the inquest but out of deference to you and your tender feelings, I didn't go. But I can read and what I see with my own eyes does not make nice reading. This is not hearsay, mother, as I'm sure you'd like to suggest. What it amounts to in the way I read between the lines of the witnesses is a strong suggestion that you contributed to Dad's death in ways that are entirely in keeping with your character as a beautiful ice queen, haughty and with your mind made up like a steel trap. Dad didn't stand a chance with you when it came to reason, logic and common sense. You are not a person that anyone can have a sensible debate with. He had feelings and not so well hidden under his exterior was a soft and sensitive inner self that called for sympathy and understanding from a loving supportive wife instead of a dragon-like person who can only see things her way."

"Oh, my God. I don't have to take any more of this," screamed an angry Kathy.

Kathy had already discussed the situation with Alan, who had not previously known that his father was transsexual until the Sadlers explained the condition. The boy was shocked at first but after a patient explanation he had accepted his father's dilemma and could see how David felt himself to be in a trap.

"I imagine the psychiatrist told you a few home truths, judging by the transcript," suggested Elaine who was quite prepared in case Kathy became violent. "Why don't you ask Alan what he thinks?"

"It has nothing to do with you, Alan, and I forbid you to get into this fight," Kathy shouted.

"All right cool it, Mom," said Alan. "What Elaine has said is quite believable particularly after reading the transcript. I think I can understand the reasons why he decided to kill himself, gruesome though it was. The thing that pisses me off is the way you treat his sister, Aunt Elizabeth and Uncle Tom. Only a blind man would have failed to see the way you snubbed them at the funeral. They've always been very kind to Elaine and me and, were particularly nice while I stayed with them after Dad's death. What's the big deal here? Why can't you be friends?"

"It's none of your damned business, but one day you'll understand, but until then I don't want to hear their name in this house." Tom Sadler handled the investment portfolio of the Rakewood estate and Kathy comforted herself with a mental note that she must get that changed. The argument only ended when Kathy made her way to her bedroom, slammed the door and promptly fell into her pillows, bursting into tears. Both her kids had touched some sensitive nerves and in her heart of hearts she knew they were right, although it would be a long time before she would admit it.

* * * * *

Part II

The Transformation

Chapter Four

An Impossible Dream

Jack Dempster lay sleepless beside his wife Moira. He felt jealous of the fact that she could sleep through almost anything, and at any time she wished. Rclaxation was something which came naturally to her. By comparison he was always on edge, anticipating something which haunted him and there were several factors in his life capable of haunting him and one or two that terrified him.

It was about 3 a.m. when Jack glanced at his bedside clock. He knew that for the past four hours he had been laying there, more or less sleepless, wound up like a clockwork motor unable to be released. He thought that maybe he did drop off in a light restless sleep, but it was as though Morpheus just touched him and allowed a few minutes of what he thought had been sleep as he came too once again with a jolt. He tossed and turned and eventually decided to get up, make a cup of tea and read a chapter or two in his current book. He did this to take his mind off the subject which was keeping him awake.

After two cups of tea, several cookies and two hours of reading and a visit to the toilet, he at last felt drowsy enough to go back to bed, knowing that by now he would be lucky to have two hours of sleep before the alarm clock went off. Moira would get up with him when the alarm sounded. She had slept well and felt fully refreshed after her shower. She was concerned when Jack told her how bad a night he had suffered.

"What kept you awake, dear?" she asked over breakfast. She was full of concern because these sleepless nights without explanation seemed to occur too frequently. Jack said he didn't know, except that he had an attack of what he called "over-active mind." His job was secure, he seemed to like his position as an engineer for which his qualifications were impeccable, and so far as she knew he had neither health or financial problems. Of their three children, they certainly had every cause for satisfaction with their two younger teenage children. Jennifer, the middle child was now in first year university, and Joshua had excellent grades in high school and planned to follow his sister upon graduation.

The oldest child was Jeremy, three years older than Jennifer. His life was in ruins due to drug addiction. He was typical of that modern day phenomenon-- the modern middle class kid from a good home, who had screwed up on drugs. He had run the gamut of everything commonly available until he ended up on heroin, a kid lost to his family and the society from which he came, totally addicted and seemingly beyond redemption with no intention or desire to ever change his life for the better. Jeremy's tragedy was no secret. Everyone in the family knew about it and were heartsick and all prayed that his life would turn around and he'd come back, but it was not something they dwelt upon even though Moira and Jack shared each other's grief. This was not the cause of Jack's sleeplessness although the thought of their flesh and blood, dirty and dishevelled and often living out in the open in all weathers, was a constant reminder. His skin pock-marked with needle scars and his face running in sores, did nothing for Jack and Moira's composure when in their warm bed or well ordered home when the image of Jeremy crossed their minds.

Jack joined the traffic into his city office, a drive usually of about 40 minutes in the morning rush hour. He was worried by a feeling of mounting pressure. He had readily admitted to his family doctor, who knew all about Jeremy, that he had everything in the conventional sense, but about three months ago he had made a critical decision.

Somehow he knew that he had to face his problem head on, as the pressure was becoming unbearable. He was far from understanding it all and why he of all people, had been selected by God or nature to carry this burden. The secret, which had borne him down for most of his life, felt as though it was now forcing its way out into the open almost like an uncontrollable growth of some sort. His doctor had referred him to a psychiatrist and it was to this Dr. Margaret Myers that Jack had finally made as complete a revelation of his problem as he knew how.

"My problem, Doctor," he blurted out early in the interview, "is that I've always wished that I had been born female. I can't understand it, but I first became aware of this strange feeling before I even went into Grade 1 at school. I've read of people describing themselves as 'being a woman trapped in a man's body' and that is how I often feel. Sometimes it's worse than having a severe and endless nagging pain or toothache. At least one can have a tooth pulled, but there seems no answer to this. The worst thing is that I'm under the constant stress of worrying what will happen to my wife and children, my home and my job if I can't find a proper answer and somehow deal with it in the best interests of us all including myself."

"That's pretty typical," replied Dr. Myers. "You're suffering from a classic case of gender dysphoria which wakens up many mixed emotions, including guilt and anxiety over family matters. You've mentioned your oldest son and his drug problems, but you've done the best you can for the boy so don't blame yourself for that. Jeremy seems to have always been a problem even as a small child by what you tell me. Some kids seems to be preprogrammed for this kind of life, despite the best that the parents can do for them, in a loving parent and child relationship."

"Jeremy has already blamed Moira and me for all his troubles, so that's not new. But what will my friends think if they ever find out about this transsexuality? They'll shun me like a leper? Will I ever be able to look my wife in the eye again and tell her that I love her -- with any hope that she will ever believe me? Will she reject me as a queer, a weirdo and a person having known for almost all my life that a problem existed within me? I don't think I can blame her if she feels that I kidded her into our marriage. What's just as worrying is that the other two kids are into the most critical years of their education and to my mind the last thing they need to disturb their current security is the knowledge that their father harbours these thoughts. Yet, I feel that I may eventually be forced by the pressures within to confront the whole mess head on and take some sort of action."

Dr. Myers listened patiently to Jack, by now in tears as he slowly managed to unburden himself of his worries and anxieties. Now and again she would quietly slip in a question, when it appeared that Jack was going off on a tangent or when she wanted Jack to enlarge on some train of thought which was developing. The psychiatrist helped by putting Jack as much as possible at his ease, as she formulated her initial opinion that here was a classic case of a transsexual, a self-disciplined man who, being highly principled felt his duties and obligations keenly, a man who had performed normally through his life, had married and had fathered children, and now felt himself to be in danger of losing it all. Now his stress and anxiety was obviously so severe that he felt he was being torn to pieces by the conflict between his mind and his body, his female presence and his male reality.

Dr. Myers knew that any suggestion that Jack should just forget all about it and get on with his life like any other good heterosexual man was worse than useless. When a sufferer from the condition had reached this far and found it necessary to unburden himself, it was probably too late to head his problem off, even if it was possible, which in the light of experience was extremely unlikely. Whether anything could have been done earlier would never be known as Jack had found it impossible to share his secret with anyone. It was the nature of the condition, with so many negative factors. He had experienced the mystery, the shame, the feeling of walking into quicksands and an inability to communicate sometimes so severe as to make him feel bound and gagged.

"I simply don't know where to start talking about this. If I told my wife that I thought the only answer for me was that I should change sex, she would go clean through the roof. If she felt that everything she relied on as part of her own role in life was being cut away from underneath her, I couldn't blame her for one moment," added Jack.

"Do you realize, Mr. Dempster, that today you've just taken one first critical step in resolving your problems?" noted Dr. Myers.

"Oh, what's that?" asked Jack, a little taken aback.

"For the first time in your life, by what you tell me, you've been able to communicate with a fellow human being on this subject. Previously you've been all bottled up in a state of total repression and now, because someone else shares your secret, you already feel a little better about it all."

Jack agreed. Perhaps a better word was relieved, but whatever, he had taken a first big step forward for himself. He knew he had to do something as he could not tread water for ever. If he tried to it could only mean one thing, the condition would eventually drown or kill him, or at least its side effects would.

The appointment terminated, a referral was made to an associate of Dr. Myers for a second opinion. "After you've seen my colleague, Dr. George Fellowes, we'll get together again and see where we go from there."

* * * * *

Two weeks later Jack had an appointment with the second psychiatrist. Dr. Fellowes had a pleasant, easy-going disposition and from the beginning Jack felt relaxed and more able to speak out. They followed the usual routine of questions and answers and Jack half expectantly, half hoped that Dr. Fellowes would pass an opinion there and then. Was he a transsexual or was he not? At least if he was diagnosed transsexual he would know where he was at. He recalled that Dr. Myers had described his condition as being gender dysphoria, but was this the same thing as transsexualism? He wasn't sure because he still didn't properly understand the phenomenon, but if some other result came up he might have felt relieved. But what then? He did not like the idea of a fresh set of problems just when he felt he was breaking through on the one he was most conscious of, with which at last he was starting to feel slightly more confident.

Dr. Fellowes focussed far more on Jack's professional background and career than did Dr. Myers. He wanted to test to what extent Jack had thought out the future in terms of maintaining his career and earning capacity in the event that a gender change turned out to be the right course for him.

"I haven't really thought out a game plan yet, Doctor. My mind has been more like a seething can of worms. Any logical plan for containing the worst effects of this affliction have so far not been my top priority. I've exhausted myself just fighting this serpent back into the inner recesses of my mind. But after meeting Dr. Myers and yourself, things do seem to be coming a little clearer. What you have asked me about my future is certainly something I'll have to give thought to. I think I've been more controlled by all the imaginary reactions of people and what they will think and say. Too often my imagination has functioned in the worst and most negative terms. I imagine my wife screaming at me, my kids spitting on me and my whole family shunning me. Y'know its a wonderful thing to have and be a part of a united, supportive and loving family and I guess we all take it for granted until some sort of crack appears to shake up one's security. What's caused me so much of a nightmare is the thought of all this going down the drain and me ending up with nothing, a lost son, no one to love, no loving family around me, drifting without a future and nowhere to go. It's a pretty horrible prospect to contemplate."

Dr. Fellowes was sympathetic. "You mention your lost son and here you are fighting against the recognition that you may have a bereavement in the family, but don't give up hope. You haven't driven him to drugs. He has fallen, yes, of his own volition into the habit. It's one of the greatest problems in our society and for it you cannot take on all the burdens of society generally.

"I know Jack, how your mind has been working overtime on your problems. Our role is to help you calm down and free yourself of the panic attacks and relieve the nagging pain. We can never cure a condition like this in the sense of giving you something for an infection or an attack of flu. What we do is try to guide you back to higher ground, rebuild your confidence and increase your sense of security within yourself. Some psychiatrists might describe it as helping keep your wheels on track so that you don't derail. However, one might think of it, the idea is to help you cope with your challenges. This does not inevitably mean a change of sex. Some can handle it without going that far, but others eventually reach the conclusion that this is the only answer for them. We never tell you to go ahead on our initiative. Our main concern is to guide you until you tell us that you are ready to take the final irreversible steps. There's no miraculous cure, but there can be a happy effective ending to it all."

* * * * *

In his anxiety Jack had developed a hiatus hernia. Coffee, alcohol and spices were out of the question as they only increased the acid and gave him heartburn. With medication the hernia would calm down so that he could then handle a fairly normal diet. When anxiety and stress built up, he would again feel quite ill as the hernia became active. He found bland foods became boring and for relief he drank a lot of milk.

When he was into one of these cycles, Moira knew that he was disturbed, but enquire as she would she could never pin down what it was that so gravely upset him. It was not Jeremy as his situation was completely out in the open and in any event, Jack and she completely understood that situation and acted in unison with each other. Jack blamed it on business, but when she made discrete enquiries with friends at his place of work, they knew of nothing specific to cause him such worry.

Eventually she had to conclude that it was something in his basic body chemistry, so she did not pursue the subject very openly in order to avoid upsetting him needlessly. When Jack found himself in this state of mind he knew the best antidote was to revert to the fantasy world in his mind. This often took place while lying in bed awake for hours on end. What Jack was experiencing was something common among transsexuals; an escape from reality and a transference of the mind to another world which he could experience through his fantasy. He would think of himself as a born female and run through his mind all the experiences that he imagined a girl growing up would go through and the challenges that an adult woman would face. In the end he would tell himself that it plainly boiled down to the one simple fact -- he had been born in the wrong sex and it was a matter of trying to push a square peg into a round hole.

The effect it had on his sleep pattern was very disturbing. With so little sleep during the night he was often dozing off at work or with the family. Often it was a tough, slogging experience as he did his utmost to keep his mind on the task in hand. Moira had become used to her husband sleeping for two hours following dinner. It was no fun for her and at times became a positive embarrassment particularly when they had guests and Jack would drowse off to sleep. Moira knew something had to be done about this. Jack looked drawn and grey at times and at this rate she could see his health being permanently undermined.

* * * * *

Following one of his frequent bouts of sleeplessness, Jack was sitting in his dressing gown sipping a cup of hot lemon with a dash of rum. He hoped it would soothe him and help him to return to sleep. He wondered what he could read and scanned the contents of a nearby bookcase. His eyes lighted on an old family photo album which had been sitting there seemingly undisturbed for years. If anyone ever looked at it he had never seen them doing so.

He pulled the album down and noted that it concerned itself with the Dempster family and their relatives. There were long dead grandparents and great grandparents and single shots of young bachelors and maiden aunts in their youth. Obviously by their style of dress and the aged sepia and daguerreotype prints, many were people from the Victorian age. He could not be certain of their identity, but made a note that he should ask his father, before he passed away and took this personal knowledge with him.

As he thumbed through towards the end of the album he recognized his father as a boy standing with his parents and sisters in a family group taken on their Saskatchewan farm. The eldest in a family of four, Hugh Dempster already showed the proud bearing that never left him through the rest of his life. A later photo showed him in Royal Canadian Air Force uniform as a recently graduated pilot officer standing beside his Hurricane fighter plane. Hugh was to go through the Battle of Britain and the war in Europe, bringing down his share of enemy planes and surviving two ditchings himself. Hugh came out of the RCAF after the war with a Distinguished Flying Cross – the DFC, and the rank of Squadron-Leader. He married his childhood sweetheart, Mary Manning, the daughter of another local farming family.

The Dempster and Manning families were surprised when Hugh announced his intention of joining the Royal Canadian Mounted Police. Old Bob Dempster's long-cherished hope was that his son would be taking over the farm with its hundreds of rolling acres of wheat. Bob saw it as a fitting reward for a fighting man who had returned to his homeland a hero, but this was not to be. Hugh's instincts were with the military way of life and when that phase ended it seemed perfectly natural to him that he would choose the para-military RCMP. Jean Dempster, Jack's grandmother, was to die first only to be followed a year later by Bob. The farm was sold and the proceeds divided between Hugh and his sibling sisters all of whom were to marry by the mid-1950s.

Hugh took to police work like a duck to water. His transfer to British Columbia followed several years working with detachments across the prairies during which one more brother to Jack and two sisters were born. When Hugh arrived to take up an appointment in the Fraser Valley he was already a corporal and a man singled out for promotion as he worked hard at course after course. More and more he specialized in detective work and eventually retired as a superintendant in charge of the detective division.

Jack continued to thumb through the pages to see pictures of himself with his brother Herbert and sisters Margaret and Marion through the various stages of growing up and graduating. Margaret, the elder sister did not develop any significant career, and married quite young. Her husband became a school teacher and Herbert followed in his father's footsteps in the RCMP.

Marion chose a nursing career and was still single. She of all of them was most like their father having a single-minded interest in her career which she pursued with the determination that had been typical of Hugh Dempster, starting up after his wartime flying career.

Jack wondered how all his family members would take the news of his transsexualism, but his father was the one he most worried about. Hugh had developed in the tradition of "an officer and a gentleman." He was not given to ready acceptance of liberal points of view. His country, the reigning monarch, the national anthem, the flag and Remembrance Day were all of great importance in his scheme of things. Even after he became a plain clothes detective, he loved the odd occasion, such as Remembrance Day, when he could get all decked out in his best dress uniform of which he was infinitely proud. Hugh Dempster was a royalist and a patriot, who described himself as an Anglo-Canadian when people started to brag about their Irish, Welsh or Scottish or any other ancestry. When it came to traditions and respect for the ruling authority he fully expected his family to follow his line of thinking and, in most important regards they did exactly that.

There was the photo of brother Herbert when he married Maureen Stanley. Known by all simply as "Bert" he looked smart in his R.C.M.P. uniform. This again was like a military wedding, with Bert's best man and the groom's father in full dress uniform. Bert and Jack had grown up almost like a pair of twins, but Jack, the older by two years, was quiet and thoughtful and not a keen player of aggressive boy's games. How Bert would receive Jack as his new sister was a question upon which Jack could only speculate and, when he did, it made him tremble as he knew that Bert was a reincarnation of his father.

Margaret, who was quite intellectually inclined and more like Jack in her attitudes, married Frank Frostad, the son of a Norwegian fishing family from Richmond, B.C.. After working on family fishing boats for a few years, Frank decided on a career as a school teacher. He liked the sea but wanted something more steady. He used his savings from several good fishing seasons to put himself through university. Jack wondered how they would react to the news? He speculated in his mind, as they were not close to Moira and himself and unlike Bert and Maureen they didn't see each other too often. This was perhaps natural enough when Frank was appointed vice-principal at a high school in a far northern British Columbia town.

Marion, the youngest of his siblings, was the one Jack felt might be the most accepting. As a trained nurse her specialist knowledge might help her understand it all better. She had access to research papers and medical texts and books galore. She had always shown that she had an enquiring mind and if she found herself lacking in knowledge on anything she always took steps to find out. How she might react to Jack's news should it come out into the open was again questionable, but of all of them he knew he would tell her first, when and if the time came.

Jack started to feel drowsy and quietly returned to his bed. Moira was sleeping, but returned to a moment of consciousness when turning over. She mumbled "Are you okay, Darling?" and returned to her slumbers. Oh, to be able to sleep like a log as Moira did! No wonder she was always bright and breezy each morning while he felt he had to drag his feet around for the first half hour after awakening. This constant anxiety was really too much and he wondered how much longer he could take it before it started to seriously undermine his health. He dozed off thinking that something had to be done about it, but exactly what he was uncertain. He disliked the idea of sleeping pills, but would ask Dr. Myers for an anti-depressant next time he saw her,

The fact that he had consulted Dr. Myers was a big step and he looked forward to his next appointment with her. She seemed, at this stage, to be the only connection of which he could feel certain. She exuded quiet confidence and no matter what he had raised with her she had responded with a knowledgeable answer. Even though he had only had the one appointment with her, it was good to have someone like her in his camp. She had allayed his fears to a great extent and he felt better after visiting her.

* * * * *

Jack did what he occasionally did. He parked his car in his allotted space at his office and then walked from there into the Downtown Eastside. He was looking for his son, Jeremy. His addiction had started when the boy was in high school, probably almost innocently by trying marijuana and then progressively moving on to more destructive drugs, like heroin. Jack and Moira had been watchful for signs of this kind of thing, as Jeremy had always been the difficult one among the three children. He had played truant on a number of occasions and by comparison with his sister and brother his grades throughout school had been poor. He'd had to be watched in another way as if left to his own devices he was quite capable of unmerciful bullying of his younger siblings. Perhaps it was because of bullying that he never built up any great affection from the two younger ones. Joshua and Jennifer tended to stand together and maybe there was an element of mutual protection in that.

Jeremy developed the habit of leaving home for a few days and then returning to deal with items like laundry and bathing. Any complaint from his parents was deflected by ignoring them. As if to add to the lack of direct communication, Jeremy would respond by holding up his hand and say, "Here, talk to my hand." Eventually, after much heart-searching and recurring thefts of money and household possessions, Jack and Moira had confronted Jeremy and told him that he was no longer allowed to come home. Any accusation to do with theft was strenuously denied.

"If something is missing how come you don't blame Josh or Jen?"

"We don't blame them because we know they're not guilty," said Moira, "And we know you're on drugs. You're hooked on a habit and the stealing you do is to buy drugs. It's a common pattern."

"Bullshit, I'm nuthin' of the sort," replied a hostile Jeremy.

"Well, what are you then? What sort of work are you doing? How do you pay your way through life?" asked Jack who mentally noted how his son's manner of speech had deteriorated and how prone he was to common vulgarities.

"Mind your own Goddamned business."

"No, we're not minding our own Goddamned business, as you put it. So long as you think you have the right to enter this home and use it whenever you think it suits you for whatever purpose, then it's our business," replied Moira with great firmness.

"Anyone I know needs food in his belly and some sort of shelter over his head. Just how do you survive?" asked Jack.

"I get by," came the surly response.

"Yeah, I know by hook or by crook and it'll be a helluva a lot of the last." Jack knew he was sounding mean, but he also knew as a parent that he had to stand firm. His addicted son's personality and appearance had changed so much in the past year as to make him almost like another person.

"Don't give me that shit, Dad, You know fucking well how I get by without me having to spell it out."

"Yeah, I know all right. Drug addicts like you have no future and simply exist from one fix to the next. You get by, by lying and stealing and no doubt by shaking people down in one way or another. You know Jeremy, that this is the saddest thing that any parent can endure. To see our own flesh and blood reduced to the status of an unwanted deadbeat. A felon without hope and with only two ends in view. That's more than likely a long spell in jail or an early death."

"Oh, I can give it up any time I want"

"Now, it's your turn to hand out the shit, as you put it," said Moira. "Jeremy, you're hopelessly addicted and no amount of persuasion is going to ever change your mind, until you yourself come to the decision that you want to give it up. If you live long enough that might take many years, during which time you'll go to hell and back many times over."

"Yeah, just like you Mom to always have to add an 'as you put it' to the end of a statement. That's a typical middle-class put-me-down to those less fortunate with less education and all that shit," replied a suddenly vehement Jeremy.

Jeremy turned away not wanting to meet the eyes of either of his parents. "What's the matter Jer? I guess your mother's remarks are hitting home and you can't take the heat," said Jack.

"I'm going. I can see I'm not wanted here. Everything about this fucking house gives me the creeps."

"I can understand that," said Jack. He reached into his pocket and gave Jeremy the coins for his street car fare. "Here's your car fare. Take it and get out of here and don't come back until you can honestly tell us that you want to clean up your life and get it back on track. You know we're here to help when you can show us it won't be time wasted and money misspent. Until then don't come back."

Jeremy gathered his few belongings and made to leave. The money Jack had put on the kitchen table lay there. Moira took his arm as she said, "We'll shed many tears believe me, but helping you in your present condition is an impossibility." She attempted to give him a kiss on the cheek but he pulled himself away, grabbed the change and stormed out.

* * * * *

Jack remembered that scene of a year ago. He played it back in his mind as he walked east towards Main and East Hastings. He was dressed in his old gardening clothes, anything better might have looked out of place. As he walked he glanced at the human wrecks who hung around, their minds in another drug-induced world. A dealer walked up to Jack assuming he was looking for drugs. The man said nothing as he held out a small white package. Jack replied, "Not today thanks," as he walked on. Prostitutes tried to catch his eye, but Jack avoided eye contact, as he glanced into alcoves and down lanes.

Jack had been here before as this was not the first time he had sought out his son in this desolate street scene. His usual routine was to persuade Jeremy to accompany him to a local greasy spoon restaurant where he could fill him up with a hamburger and french fries. For quite a while Jeremy had tried to maintain some semblance of cleanliness, but this time it was to be different.

He spotted Jeremy leaning up against an old brick wall talking to a girl. Jeremy looked surprised when he heard before he even saw Jack.

"Hi, Jer. How's it going?"

Jeremy seemed to jump with surprise. Jack assumed that his son's nerves were on edge.

"Oh. Hi Dad. Not so good today. Not so good." There was a tremble in his voice that was so bad that it sounded like a warble and his face had suppurating sores that looked quite bad.

The girl had taken off as the conversation developed. "Can I take you for a burger, Jer?"

"You can, but I need a twenty, in the worst way."

Jack knew exactly what this was for as he took a folded bill out of his pocket. It was a moment Jack had anticipated.

"Go and get your fix, and I'll wait for you in that restaurant over there. How long are you likely to be?"

"Give me about twenty minutes."

"If you're not over there in thirty minutes, I'll be gone and you'll miss a good meal."

Jack ambled over to the restaurant and ordered a coffee, while he glanced through a much-handled copy of yesterday's morning newspaper. Soon enough Jeremy joined him. He was so dirty as to be repulsive.

"Jer, do you mind if I suggest you go to the bathroom and wash your hands?"

Jeremy looked at his filthy hands and suddenly looked a little embarrassed. "Oh yeah, Dad, I'll be right back."

"I'll order you a burger with fries, while you're away."Jack sat there glumly after giving the order to the counter girl.'What the hell are we going to do with this kid?' he thought to himself. He knew then that the only hope was to find out what agencies existed that might be able to give some help. The kid was obviously now living on the street without any proper facilities for getting a periodic cleanup. Just then Jeremy returned and tucked into his burger. It was as though he hadn't eaten for a week, although Jack knew that when on a drug binge the last thing that went through their minds was the matter of food. No wonder most of them looked like half-starved and drowned rats.

* * * * *

Chapter Five

The Clearing of Clouds

Dr. Margaret Myers had referred her file on Jack Dempster to her associate in the practice, Dr George Fellowes, for a back-up opinion. Dr. Myers was regarded within the profession as being pre-eminent in her understanding and success in helping gender dysphoria cases, but caution demanded that she always obtain a second opinion. These were people's lives she was dealing with and the last thing anyone needed was a faulty diagnosis.

"I saw Jack Dempster this morning," Dr. Fellows said over lunch. "We spent over an hour together. At first he was quite tense, somewhat defensive and overly anxious about many aspects of his family life, but after about 20 minutes he seemed to relax and I got him to talk quite freely about his past. He seems to believe that his first recollection of this strange feeling about wishing he had been born in the opposite sex goes back to around age five. There's every indication that as he grew older the conviction became more obsessive, that he was in fact a girl trapped in a male body. He thinks he did his first crossdressing experiments using his mother's and sister's belongings when he was about 12. And then he followed the classic pattern of fear and disgust and resolved to bury it all very deeply, put it out of his mind and pretended that it had never happened.

"He went to university and buried himself in his studies graduating after seven years in his branch of engineering with a

Ph.D. He's since done much in the way of post-graduate studies and has lectured and delivered research papers. He has a well-established professional reputation, but fears that all this will be ruined if his secret slips out. He met his wife following graduation. She completed a law degree but never practised. He obviously thinks the world of her and his family. The two younger children also seem to be academically bound, but the eldest is a heartbreak case for both of them."

Dr. Fellowes knew that his colleague would be familiar with all this, but it was always their practice in reporting to each other to confirm everything they had covered in writing, in case they should ever be called as witnesses. Dr. Myers took a deep breath as if she was gathering her thoughts, her colleague having summed up the situation very adequately,

"George, I take it you agree that this man is a typical transsexual."

"Oh yes, I do, and as he gets older it seems to be increasing in intensity which is also often typical as we know. Sometimes a specific event like a marital breakup might trigger a train of events that causes the condition to erupt, but I can find no specific reason for the build-up of tension and stress that Jack is obviously suffering, although his son's drug addiction has clearly not helped in any way. There is a reason I'm sure which long predates his son's problems, even if it's a matter of one anxiety feeding on the previous one in a spiral of increasing intensity," Dr. Fellowes responded.

"Well, I suppose we may find out something as we delve deeper, but what's critical now, is to ease his anxiety and give him every opportunity to discover for himself what his preferred course of action should be," said Dr. Myers. "I'll confirm to him that we consider him to be transsexual, which might relieve his mind of the constant questioning. Sometimes I believe the reassurance to a transsexual that he is now in touch with someone who understands and can identify the problem is a milestone on the road to at least giving some comfort. I can see that Mr. Dempster has many challenges ahead, occasioned by his own sense of duty, status and a dozen other things that all add up to a social and emotional tragedy in the making if he can't face up to it all and deal with his difficulties. That includes reaching a satisfactory level of understanding with his wife and family.

"He has also expressed his deep concerns about Jeremy, the one with the drug problem. He has wondered aloud if there is any connection between Jeremy's sickness with drugs and his own gender dysphoria, in the sense that the boy might be hiding a case of gender dysphoria. I assured him that it is very improbable, but not impossible as gender dysphoria has been known to be present in two generations. It might bear watching given the high rate of substance abuse in transsexuals and, as we know, that's often a cover up for their transsexuality until it all comes out," concluded Doctor Myers.

The two doctors agreed. A week later Jack returned to another appointment with Dr. Myers.

"Jack, I have gone over your file with Dr. Fellowes, and we both agree that you're suffering from the transsexual condition. I caution you though, that there are a lot of bridges that we have to cross in order to help you. Probably the most central question which arises is do you really want to be a woman? There are a lot of realities that have to be faced by women that men seldom fully understand. It isn't all makeup, jewelry and fine clothes, but boys and girls are different from the beginning of their life on earth. The nurturing is naturally different and stepping into a full female role in life after half a century of male upbringing will be a lot trickier than stepping out of a rowboat on the beach. I'm not suggesting that you try to give me an answer to that at this stage. In all honesty you have a condition which is unlikely to go away because it is always a lifetime condition even when hidden away."

Jack seemed to breath a sigh of relief, as if to say we are now getting somewhere.

"You are responsible, respected and highly qualified," Doctor Myers went on. "You have a lot to lose should you find that the only choice you have is to go for a sexchange. Your marriage won't survive as two people of the same sex cannot remain married*, though it is possible that you and your wife will remain the best of friends. Your children's perception of you will change. You'll remain their biological father, but they, particularly your youngest boy, may feel that spiritually they have lost their father even though girls tend to handle it better. How well they adjust will depend greatly on your own attitude and whatever support you can get from your wife. You should recognise that many otherwise loving wives turn violently negative when confronted with your condition. It simply turns all their preconceptions upside down including their belief that they have a stake in an ongoing marriage which only becomes an issue when everything is suddenly placed at risk. It's a lot like dependent children who are suddenly confronted with the certainty of losing a beloved parent through a terminal illness," said Dr. Myers. Jack sat their silently. He felt he was in a daze as the doctor recited a number of truths rather like navigating through a rockbound channel on a boat. What he was hearing did not fill him with concerns, it was more a matter of feeling euphoric as at last he could see signs of clearing in the clouds that had beset him for so long.

"The most critical relationship of all is with your wife. Don't forget that she can be your strongest support or, on the law of more likely averages, your most destructive critic. The only advice I can give at this point is that you always adopt the course of utmost honesty. People respect honesty far more and they detest feeling that they have been, or are being, hoodwinked," concluded Dr. Myers.

* Legal same sex marriages have been performed in British Columbia and Ontario since 2003, following a decision of the Ontario courts.

"Well, you've certainly given me a lot to think about Doctor," Jack said. "I know that this can't be cured by some magic pill and I realise I really only have two choices. The first is to try to contain it and live with it for the rest of my life, or come clean and face up to it. Either way will take its toll, as it already has done, on me and my health. It's negative influences are bound to affect my family, as it affects the way I behave and think in an unknown number of subtle ways.

"The second route, the full sex-change, I think is bound to be destructive. My children's sense of security is likely to be undermined. My wife wants a man, not another woman sharing her bed and her life. I know you can't tell me what to do as if I have a bad case of flu. I know I have to be the ultimate decision maker."

"That's a very intelligent perception of your state at this point in your life, Jack," replied Dr. Myers. "I can't honestly say which is right for you. We can only describe the effects and-circumstances as we perceive them, based on our professional knowledge and experience. I'm glad you seem to understand that. I know you've given years of thought to this and it is now for you to assess your next moves. You have to face your situation honestly and straightforwardly. We're always here to help, to counsel, and try to keep you out of trouble. Never forget that. What you should now do is take each of your challenges, wife, children, job, future security and examine each as realistically as you know how. Whatever you do involves major decisions."

* * * * *

The disturbing case of the death by suicide of David Rakewood hit the local headlines. Rakewood had died in a fiery crash in his car. The police reports suggested evidence of a suicide, but no details had been released beyond the statement that Rakewood was understood to have been under a lot of strain in his personal life and the outcome of an enquirywas awaited.

Jack Dempster knew David Rakewood mainly through business, his firm having undertaken some engineering assignments for Rakewood Fabricators on items like steel staircases and other structural components which they were fabricating for large construction jobs. In turn, Rakewood's firm was also a frequent bidder on contracts which Dempster's firm was supervising.

Socially, Jack and Moira knew the Rakewoods mostly by repute. They knew the Rakewoods circulated in the uppermost strata of local society, a type of social life which did not appeal to the Dempsters with their much quieter, less ostentatious values. To appear in the society columns would have left them cold. They would have regarded such attention on the part of the media as being an unwarranted interference with their private lives. As a consequence Jack Dempster did not view the opinions on transgendered subjects, held by his contemporaries with the same degree of horror as David Rakewood would have. Dempster's concern above all, had to do with the relationship with his wife, children and close family.

Living as both families did on the west side of the city in fairly close proximity to each other, it was not so surprising that the two wives would come to meet each other. Usually it was a passing word and a pleasant smile as their shopping carts passed each other in the aisle at the supermarket. The Dempster's knew Rakewood's sister, Elizabeth, and her husband, Tom Sadler, far better. They were near neighbours and Elizabeth and Moira frequently got together for a morning coffee. The two couples came into contact with each other at parent-teacher meetings, at social gatherings in the neighbourhood and enjoyed the occasional dinner together.

Jack was reading from the local newspaper over breakfast with his wife when he came across the report of Rakewood's death."I wonder what brought all that on. My understanding was that he had everything going for him in this life: great wife and family, nice home, a prosperous business. I suppose it might have been depression over a health problem or some such thing."

Jack was not to know how close he had come to the mark until he and Moira returned from their Hawaiian vacation some weeks later.

"I should send her a card or something" said Moira. "I don't know her well enough to phone and quite likely the last thing she wants is to hear from all sorts of people. Coping with family and close friends will be enough, I'm sure. Maybe I should phone his sister Elizabeth. She'll be concerned as she was very fond of her brother."

* * * * *

Later, Jack was discussing the suicide with Ben Dawson, a colleague, over brief morning coffee at their office. Dawson remarked. "I knew Dave and his wife quite well. They'd really developed into dreadful snobs. I'm not sure which one led the way, although I suspect it was her with her set of phoney values. My wife said they had 'an exclusive club complex' and they considered themselves to be very special and only able to move in the upper echelons of society. I guess when you get high enough in the pecking order of things, the fall, when it comes, is much more dramatic."

"I never got that impression with Dave, who always struck me as being very democratic at work where I knew him best, but he certainly couldn't have made it any more dramatic. Jumping off the Lions Gate Bridge is dramatic enough for most, but to do it in your car is almost like cremating one of the ancient Viking chiefs by setting his ship adrift and turning it into a funeral pyre. I wonder if David was trying to send some message. Why didn't he just go into the trees and hang himself or blow his brains out? The bottom line would have been the same," Jack replied.

"I don't suppose we'll ever know, although the inquest might answer a lot of the mysterious questions which are going the rounds. It's the kids I'm concerned about. It could be quite damaging to them. His son goes to the same school as my two lads who say that he's been so upset he's had to stay out of school since the suicide. Dave was known to be heavily on the bottle and for that there had to be a reason. Some have suggested that it was business worries, but Simon Guthrie, his lawyer friend, told me that there was no such problem. The business was in good shape and making lots of money, although others really ran it for him." said Ben.

Jack felt very much inclined to let the conversation drop at this point so made moves to leave the table. Somehow he felt that Ben was probing a little too much and loose tongues and speculation only gave rise to more rumour. "Look at the time," said Jack as he glanced at his watch. "I've got to get back to my office, I'm expecting some clients in quite soon."

Jack felt quite upset as he sat at his desk, ostensibly looking through some documents he had prepared in anticipation of the arrival of his clients. He was reading the sheaf of papers, but was not taking in what his eyes saw. His mind was dwelling on David Rakewood as he thought of his fiery death. Occasionally Jack had felt suicidal when he sensed that he was caught in a one-way trap. He wanted to go back but couldn't. There seemed to be no escape from his dilemma as circumstances seemed to be moving him forward inexorably towards a destiny which bristled with traps for the unwary. Why not just end it all, he thought, but how? He knew that Rakewood's method was not the one for him. Maybe he should buy a handgun of some sort and hide it away in case of future need. No, that was ridiculous. It was no answer and would only leave his wife and children stranded emotionally and always wondering about the necessity for an act of such finality. And then there was Jeremy.

There was a buzz on the intercom.

"Mr. Assiz is here to see you, Mr. Dempster," said the receptionist at the front desk.

"Okay, show him through please." Jack shook himself together and was all business once again. This was an important contract covering the construction of a new mosque and community centre. He stood to receive his client who was a prominent member of the Ismaili sect of the Muslim religion. Ismailis were followers of the Aga Khan and formed a distinct wealthy and well-educated group centred in Vancouver. The Ismailis pursued their good works quietly and without ostentation. Jack's firm had worked with them on several occasions and he greatly admired the quietly, good natured manner in which they conducted their lives.

Mr. Assiz communicated with the aid of many pleasantries. Jack went over the contracts and asked Assiz to take them away to go over them with his colleagues. If everything was in order he would put out an invitation to tender.

After Mr. Assiz left, Jack thought for some minutes on his own religious values. What was it that made a man like Mr. Assiz so quietly content and serene and in such contrast to himself? One answer which was obvious to Jack, was that Assiz was content with his manhood and undoubtedly the spiritual values of his faith bolstered this up. The Dempsters attended church from time to time, but would hardly be classified as keen United Church members, the denomination to which they belonged. He thought to himself that he would have to consider this. Maybe he should seek a confidential meeting with his minister to explore the possibilities of a religious answer to his transsexualism. Maybe there was an essential cog missing from his make-up and there may be an answer through religion or spiritual deliverance.

* * * * *

Jack phoned the Reverend George Marley, his local United Church minister. He knew him but slightly through exchanging pleasantries when the minister stationed himself at the door of the church following a Sunday morning service.

"Sure, come on in, Mr. Dempster. If you're free Wednesday evening let's meet at the rectory office at say 8.00 pm. We can then take our time."

Rev. Marley wondered what it was that Jack Dempster had on his mind. To say the least he was a less-than-common visitor and certainly not one he would ever describe as a keen churchgoer.

Jack had mentioned to Moira that he had this appointment. She was curious, but did not press him. "I simply want to have the opportunity of exploring my spiritual values," he said. "There are times when I feel an essential element is missing in my life which might have something to do with my anxiety and lack of sleep." Beyond that he gave his wife no hint.

The meeting with Rev. Marley was relaxing as they drank tea and nibbled on cookies brought in by Mrs. Marley. Jack wondered about the life of a minister. Everything seemed so unhurried and serene. Mrs. Marley formed the perfect picture of the contented supportive wife, always, no doubt, at her husband's beck and call to perform small, but not unimportant duties like serving tea to guests on their best chinaware. He wondered what their sex life was like or if there even was, or ever had been, a sex life. Maybe they had risen above that common human need.

Jack had never addressed Rev. Marley by his given name, but was invited to do so now. "Call me George, and I take it I may call you Jack?" said Rev. Marley who was perhaps 10 years older than Jack.

"Certainly, certainly," replied Jack warming up to this most pleasant of men. He supposed to himself that to do God's work effectively one must be a superb diplomat.

After a brief pause to fill teacups and pass the cookies the question that Jack wanted to pose came to the fore.

"Well, Jack, what brings us together this evening? I've known you for years as a member of the congregation, but I can't recall an occasion when we did anything more than holding the Communion cup to your lips and shaking hands at the door after service."

"That's perfectly true," replied Jack. "I wanted to get together with you because I'm exploring every avenue I can think of in dealing with a highly personal problem. You see, er-er-George, I'm a medically diagnosed transsexual and whether I like it or not, I'm being propelled along a course to which there seems only one final answer."

George Marley's slight smile never left his face. "That's a problem all right, particularly when you have a wife and children. I can understand that it has many complications. The churches have discussed the subject at some length without any positive conclusions, beyond the statement that it's a psychological illness which should be dealt with by psychological methods. I've had no personal experience with the subject in any of my congregation, but a fellow minister of our church and I have discussed the subject fairly extensively. There is at least one transsexual in his congregation who has approached him for advice.

"Church dogma, depending on which denomination is involved, tends to have its wheels stuck in a rut over this subject, but enough is known about the subject to say that it shouldn't be condemned as irrational, bizarre behaviour and I support the view that it is, in fact, biological in origin and occurs because of some malfunction in the pregnancy process. That being said, Jack, why don't you take over and tell me all about your own history. I promise not to interrupt."

Jack gave a full description of everything he knew and had experienced and detailed the consultations he had had with Margaret Myers. He described a marriage which in every way appeared to be near ideal. He was happy with, but concerned for, his children and he had few concerns about his career. He mentioned Jeremy as being the heartbreak of Moira's and his own life. He was near tears as he carried on. "I have this other being within me. She's another personality. I like her because she is always there to give me the only comfort I can get when I need it, but I hate her almost at the same time for even being present. She's like a shadow cast by the sun except that she never leaves me even when there's no sunshine to cast a shadow. The worst thing is that the older I get the more obsessive it all becomes. Short of suicide I can only see one conclusion."

"Oh, and what's that?" asked the Reverend Marley.

"I have to face it if I'm ever to have any peace. I have to go through with a gender change and, in so doing, risk everything. But better that than doing away with myself like an acquaintance of mine did recently."

"Was that anyone I know?" Mr. Marley asked.

"You might know him; David Rakewood who lived not too far from here on Sunset Drive. I don't know what was bothering him, but something serious must have undermined him to justify going out like a blazing comet," Jack replied.

"I knew him slightly as they occasionally came to my church. Was he transsexual?" asked Mr. Marley.

"Not that I know of. I suppose it could've been one of a dozen reasons."

"Getting back to you, Jack. I don't see this as being an anti-religious issue. Transsexualism is not condemned by any biblical word that I know of and there's nothing in law to prevent you dealing with the matter. Everyone has his, or her own, interpretation of right and wrong in religious and moral terms and many of us harbour prejudices we neither understand or can even define. We all have the opportunity to make our peace with God. Some interpret this very broadly while others have a more doctrinaire approach, but you can't let your life be ruled by other people's prejudices. Provided you've properly dealt with your marital and family obligations and have made adequate and honourable provisions for their security financially and emotionally, it then remains for you to deal with the health aspects of your life as best you can -- after all would anyone criticise you if you dealt with a cancerous growth or tuberculosis in order to prolong your life. Tell me one thing, though, what brought about your need to speak to me?"

Jack thought for a moment as he framed his words to honestly portray his thoughts. "Well, it came through to me after meeting with a client who belonged to the Aga Khan's Ismaili sect, that this man, seemed so relaxed and serene and content with his lot in life. He was working for his community and obviously obtaining much satisfaction from it. I'm not suggesting that I want to become a member of his sect or even a Muslim. He radiated something that I sensed more than I could actually see. He struck me as a spiritually fulfilled man in so much contrast to me with all my anxieties and uncertainties. My view of him helped me make up my mind that I had to reach an end to this section of the road in my life and make a radical change for the better."

"Did you want to speak to me in order to endorse your action or appease your conscience?" asked George Marley kindly.

"I suppose subconsciously, yes to both. I had to touch my own roots as a Christian, not with the idea of gaining some sort of absolution or applause, but more for reassurance from someone representing the official Church," Jack replied.

"Well, Jack, I'm sure you understand that I can't endorse your action any more than I would wish to condemn it. Our God is a compassionate God and I have a lot of compassion for people who have to face crises of all sorts and yours is as big a one as I have ever seen. That would be my response as a churchman. Privately, and as a fellow human being I have to add that you only pass this way once. You only get one chance in life so you have to make the best of it, according to your view of life. We all do it, I suppose. The only difference is that your route is far less common because of the relative rarity of the condition. But dealing with it is no less pertinent just because it's uncommon."

The two shook hands as Rev. Marley invited Jack to stay in touch and feel free to contact him at any time. "I'm very interested in your case and believe it's a subject about which the Church needs to be better informed. Maybe later on I'll invite you to address a group of our clergy."

"I hope you will," replied Jack as he waved his host goodbye.

* * * * *

When Jack arrived home he felt a great deal better after his meeting with the Rev. Marley. Moira was interested to hear how the meeting went.

"We had a nice cup of tea and munched on cookies and talked about spiritual values. The minister is a real gentleman and I will probably get to know him better over time. I feel a lot more secure and at peace in my own mind. I feel very much as though I should take a more active part in church activities. The anxiety and stress which so often besets me seems to have disappeared at least for the present. It would be nice to think that it will be a permanent retreat and I can shake off its destructive influence. Maybe through a more spiritual approach I can help Jeremy." said Jack almost whistfully.

"That sounds wonderful Jack and if this is what it takes to make you feel better about yourself then anything you do for the church will have my full support. But tell me one thing. You talk of 'its' destructive influence as though there is something specific, something identifiable which is eating at you. Can you tell me what it is?"

Jack suddenly felt quite uncomfortable and flustered. He should have known that with Moira's finely tuned, legally trained mind, a single word could be the cause of bringing down the entire facade behind which he had hidden for so long.

"No, I can't be sure just what it is. But maybe I'm getting a little closer to finding some answers to the mystery of my life."Jack's serenity had been rocked by Moira's innocent question. She knew she had touched a nerve somewhere, but decided to leave well enough alone. Ceaseless questioning would only cause Jack to retreat into his shell and push the answers further away.

* * * * *

Like many others the Dempsters had attended the Rakewood funeral. Inevitably Moira and Jack ran into Elizabeth and Tom Sadler. "We're so sorry that all this happened. It must be terrible for you all, but particularly Kathy," said Moira as she sympathised with Elizabeth.

Elizabeth was obviously quite distressed over her brother's tragic death and was quietly sobbing when the two friends embraced.

"We're going to Hawaii later this week. Can we get together after we come back?" asked Moira solicitously.

"I'd love to," replied Elizabeth. "There'll be a coroner's enquiry while you're away. It promises to be an ordeal for us all."

A little later as the Dempsters drove home Moira remarked that she thought Elizabeth seemed to be under a terrific strain. "She said that it promised to be an ordeal for the whole family. I wonder what she meant by that, Jack?"

"I've no idea, but I have the feeling that there's a great deal to come out over this entire affair. I get the feeling that there's a lot of tension in the air when anyone mentions the Rakewood name. It's almost like someone lights a match and everyone else is afraid the match will get too close to the leaking gasoline. That's the sort of tension I mean. It's as if everyone is awaiting an explosion."

"Yes, that's about the way I sense it. I think there was hidden meaning in Elizabeth's words about it being an ordeal for the whole family. It's generally well-known that there's no love lost between Kathy Rakewood and her sister-in-law. Elizabeth has called her a 'bloody bitch' on a number of occasions. Other than to shake hands with Kathy as we went out of the church, that's as close as I got. She seemed to be hiding behind those huge shades she was wearing. Come to think of it that's the first occasion when I've seen Kathy and her in-laws under the same roof. It must be a pretty tense relationship if it takes a funeral to bring them together. Anyway we shall see," said Moira as they entered their driveway and came to a stop in the carport.

Jack remarked on the two Rakewood children. "The boy looks like a fine young man in the making in his neat grey suit. I noticed that he stayed close to the Sadlers more than he did with Kathy. The girl, I heard came in from a hippie commune, which might explain her somewhat untidy appearance and unconventional attitude."

"From what Elizabeth has told me about her in the past, Elaine is her name, is something of a rebel who was very close to her father and has been a thorn in Kathy's side for quite a long time. I wonder what she'll do now that there's no father present. I hope she doesn't go overboard on this hippie thing."

* * * * *

Before leaving for Hawaii, Jack felt the urge to go to the Downtown Eastside to find Jeremy. He had done it before and found him in a dirty dishevelled condition, unwilling to talk to his father and avoiding eye contact although he had eagerly grabbed a ten or twenty dollar bill when it was handed to him. Jack knew it would go towards his next fix and would leave him just as puzzled and disturbed as ever with the reason for the destruction of his son which he could see every time he went there.

Their occasional meetings always took place on the street. Jack tried to coax Jeremy into a coffee shop to buy him a burger or some food, but the meetings always seem to end with a garbled and abusive lecture from Jeremy telling Jack to get out of his life.

"You don't belong down here, Dad, any more than I belong up in Shaughessy or Kerrisdale. This is my family down here. These people understand me and I understand them. We're all junkies and our life expectancy is short and none of us will live long enough to draw the old age pension." said Jeremy.

It was a message of despair and a sure sign that Jeremy measured his life in months rather than years. Always Jack tried to assure Jeremy that he could come home any time he liked:

"Your Mum and I love you Jeremy, just like Jennifer and Joshua do and we all miss you terribly. Come home and we'll get medical help to cure you of this sickness, the sickness that is killing you." Jack knew that there was less than a zero chance of this happening at this stage of Jeremy's life and Jack always wrestled with his conscience anytime he and Moira were going away. He felt almost as though he was doing something treacherous leaving some of his own flesh and blood down there on Skid Row surviving by the slimmest of hairlines. He was always afraid he would come back to hear of Jeremy's death from an overdose or some violent act.

This time he decided to go and see Jeremy before they left. He tried to make his presence as inconspicuous as possible. He wore his gardening clothes and parked his maroon coloured Buick in a parking lot some three or four blocks west of Main and Hastings, the heart of Vancouver's drug culture. No decent person would want to be seen there and if they were, they gave the many junkies as wide a berth as possible. To pass through was to run a gauntlet of beggers, begging for whatever they could coerce out of people to buy that next fix. The human wreckage was heartbreaking to see as one gingerly avoided stepping on spent condoms and discarded needles. Jack walked towards the throng of people to find his son talking in a dopey way to a most unattractive woman who had seen better days. The two appeared to be completely high on something. This was heartbreak alley for sure for a parent seeing their own flesh and blood in such a depraved and dirty condition. Jeremy averted his eyes when he saw his father as even then he was deeply ashamed of the condition to which he had sunk."Jeremy, my son, I want to talk to you," said Jack as firmly as he dare.

"Fuck off, Dad. I've told you before this is no place for you. You shouldn't come down here," said Jeremy in a thin wavering voice which matched the way he stood and weaved from side to side.

"Come on, let's go and have a cup of coffee," said Jack as he grasped Jeremy's thin emaciated arm. Jeremy did not seem to have the strength to resist as he shambled along besides his father. They went into a nearby coffee shop which would hardly have been Jacks's choice under anywhere near normal circumstances, but in this case it was nearby and reasonably clean. He wanted to get some food into Jeremy who was clearly close to a state of malnutrition.

Jack ordered two coffees and a large plate of fries. He figured that a burger might follow if Jeremy showed signs of being interested in the food before him. As it turned out the tasty fries aroused Jeremy's hunger, as he quickly demolished them, so Jack ordered a burger each.

They were sitting in a booth when an apparent stranger walked over to them and asked if he could join them. Actually Jack knew who this stranger was. In fact he had come with Jack in his car and then by arrangement kept Jack in sight as he sought out his son. The stranger was actually Stephen Jones, a retired sea captain and a reformed alcoholic whose sea career had been almost destroyed by his alcoholism. Jones had consulted with Doctor Fellowes, Margaret Myers' partner in practice and the doctor had encouraged him to take up volunteer community work, particularly that involving alcoholics. Jones became so successful with his mix of tough love, severe practicality and the application of emotional support at the right time, in recovering a number of people deemed lost to society, that he became known on the street as "The Miracle Worker."

Capt'n Jones, as he was widely addressed, pushed into the booth alongside Jeremy, so that Jeremy could not escape which Jack could see was very much what was on Jeremy's mind as soon as he saw Jones moving in to sit alongside him.

"If you don't mind, Sir, I have to be going," said Jeremy making a motion that he had to get out.

"Why the hurry, young feller?" said Jones. "I see you are just starting a beefburger. Relax and eat you meal and then you can go." said the captain kindly enough.

Jones reached over and offered his hand to Jack. "I think we met some time ago when you were working on a job at the first container terminal on the docks in Vancouver. Steve Jones." he said as Jack took his hand.

"Yes, I remember you. You worked for the stevedoring company who were to operate the terminal. I'm Jack Dempster and this is my son Jeremy Dempster."

Captain Jones turned to half face Jeremy as he offered his hand, but Jeremy ignored it. That did not surprise Jones as he had been fully briefed by Jack in a meeting they held several days ago in Doctor Fellowes' office. Jeremy rebuffed any further attempts by Jack or the captain to open up a conversation, by simply ignoring them as he finished off his hamburger. He wiped his mouth with the back of his hand and sleeve and then said, "If you two gentlemen will now excuse me, I have to be going."

This time they offered no resistance. Jack was holding a tightly folded twenty dollar bill between his fingers but was not about to part with it until he got his message out. Jeremy was trembling and showing some signs of needing a fresh fix as he tried to control his stomach cramps, but by now he was standing in the aisle.

"Your mother sends her love and this is from her," said Jack as he tightly held on to the twenty so that it could not be snatched. He had thought about telling Jeremy that he and Moira were going away for a holiday for a couple of weeks, but Captain Jones had earlier advised against it.

"Don't tell him anything like that Jack. That might be an invitation to a robbery or visiting your home and molesting or harassing your other two kids. When they reach the stage that Jeremy is at, they're thieves, liars and sometimes they will not stop, not even at murder to get that next fix which dominates their lives completely."

Jack had not thought of things that way but agreed that Jones was almost certainly right.

Jeremy grabbed the twenty and with barely a thank you turned on his heel and practically ran out of the cafe.

"He's off to get his next fix. Your twenty dollar bill will join all the other dirty money that the sharks will be busy relaundering by tomorrow, but I know you had to do it to get his attention."

"You got a good look at him then, Captain. Will you be able to pick him out of the crowd again?" asked Jack.

"Yes, I would. He was obviously a good looking kid at one time and with a little luck and good fortune we'll get him back, but it's going to be a hard sell all the way. I can just feel it in my bones." said Captain Jones.

"Here's how you reach me at any time." said Jack as he handed a card over with office, mobile, home and a number in Hawaii if it was necessary.

Jones was contemplative. "Don't be surprised if the police pick him up for pushing. That's how he likely covers the cost of his habit. They'll put him in the tank for long enough to at least let him dry out. If they do pick him up, let's not rush down there to bail him out. It's tough love, but a spell in the lockup won't hurt him and then we have to be there to collect him when they let him out. Otherwise they'll be waiting and will have him hooked up right away. They can't afford to lose an addict as that is how they feed their operation. I have a friendly tugboat owner with a tough skipper and mate who know all about addicts. The skipper lost a son himself a few years back. He'll make sure Jeremy gets lots of good grub, hard work and fresh air and it'll do him a world of good."

"I'll have to take your word for that," said Jack as they made their way back to the car and then to the Dempster home. Steve had left his car at Jack's and had been invited back for supper with Moira and the two younger kids. When they entered the house Moira met them with the household's two German shepherds. She knew about this little sting operation that Jack had played on their son.

"Well, how did it go?" asked Moira. Jack suggested that Captain Jones give his summary.

"It went as well as could be expected, Mrs Dempster, given the nature of the mission," said Jones. "The main thing was so that I could establish recognition for the future and that I certainly did. If Jeremy had any notion that it was a put up job he gave no hint of it, but that might dawn on him later. It's sufficient for the moment that I now know who I'm dealing with."

* * * * *

Chapter Six

A Hawaiian Interlude

After a few more sessions with Dr. Myers the pressure seemed to subside for Jack Dempster. He even found himself thinking that his gender dysphoria was all a figment of his imagination. He was more relaxed and was sleeping better and maybe, just maybe, his problem was going away. He felt that a holiday for Moira and himself was long overdue. He felt so much on top of the world. How could there be anything more idyllic than just Moira and himself enjoying a quiet beach in perfect weather on Kauai, their favourite Hawaiian island?

After their brief Hawaiian holiday they were confronted with the news of the coroner's enquiry into the death by suicide of David Rakewood. What came out was that Rakewood had died following a history not dissimilar to his own. The enquiry revealed that Rakewood was a transsexual who tried to drown his misery in alcohol. The newspaper report made no mention of the rumour that the wife had piled pressure upon pressure on the unfortunate man. This did not become apparent to the Dempsters until a little later after Moira had spoken with Elizabeth Sadler.

The effect on Jack after his first reading of the newspaper did not go unnoticed by Moira as she saw her husband go a deathly white as he read the report. She said nothing, but noticed that he had retreated to the bathroom with the newspaper and wondered why. The noise of him throwing up was only too painfully apparent.

"Honey, are you okay? Open the door," asked Moira, her voice reflecting her concern.

"I'm not sure. Maybe it was something I ate," came the reply.

Later, when she was able to get hold of the report herself she read it with rapt attention. She did recall that on several occasions, Jack had spoken some strange dialogue in his sleep which pertained to things usually of interest only to women. When she coupled this with Jack's behaviour following news of David Rakewood's transsexualism she thought it might have some relationship to her husband's hidden problem, but she hesitated to bring the subject up again.

Jack made no further mention of Rakewood's death or the verdict. As the next few weeks went by the old feelings came back, only this time they were more intense. He had told Moira nothing of his previous visitations to the psychiatrist, but with the returning anxiety there was a new one. He was starting to feel more and more dishonest about not taking her into his confidence. He knew that this time he could not put it off much longer. He had to come clean with her and the sooner the better.

He decided he would deal with it after his next appointment with Dr. Myers. He simply felt that he must have the reassurance of knowing that the doctor was still on side. He regarded the doctor as a friend in court and did not in any way want to risk turning her into a hostile witness. There was no danger of this as, after all, he was her client. But it did indicate the supreme sensitivity of a transsexual while in the process of confronting his problem.

The appointment with the doctor took on where the previous one had left off. Dr. Myers was her usual affable self, which was instantly reassuring to Jack. She wanted to know all about the events of the past two months since she had last seen him.

"Well, Doctor, things were relatively well and stable until we came back from Hawaii. First there was the news of David Rakewood's death and then came the fact, brought out at the inquest, that the man was gender dysphoric and that you had been his psychiatrist. No insult to you implied or intended, but there were so many coincidences between his history and my own, all of which have disturbed me greatly. I said to myself that there, but for the grace of God, might go I. Then all the associations, worries and shadows seemed to come back with renewed vigour. Now I know I have to break the news to my wife. How she'll take it is hard to forecast, but one thing is certain, the first reaction will be one of extreme shock and for that I'm prepared. I just hope that this is not so severe that she goes off the deep end, or totally clams up as I've heard others have, or reacts as Mrs. Rakewood is rumoured to have done. What I'd like Moira to do, and will suggest to her, is to come and see you on a one-on-one basis."

"That will be no problem, Jack. You know I'm always available. But, Jack, aside from the similarity of the Rakewood case, which was very tragic, can you think what triggered the recurrence of your dysphoria after you came back from Hawaii. If we can identify what sets it off with any specific event we might be able to understand it all the better."

"The best way I can reconstruct this in my mind is that when I came back from Hawaii, I also received the news that the government was cancelling a major contract upon which my firm was very much banking as a means of keeping our research group together. This could jeopardize everyone's future security in the firm. I was very worried and feeling very insecure when I caught the plane to Ottawa to see the Department of National Defence people. They'd made up their minds and there was to be no reprieve. When they gave me the final word I did not do what many might have and got drunk. I went out and purchased a beautiful dress and some other items, not for Moira, but for me. It was as if I was driven by some powerful irrational force to counter the anxiety provoked by the cancellation of the contract. Perhaps it was similar to how a drinker feels in seeking solace in the bottle.

"I dressed in my hotel room and found that this was the one thing that relaxed me," Jack added. "I hated looking at the news bulletins or reading the newspapers, both of which I normally pursue. As I sat there in my hotel room, crossdressed and otherwise quite relaxed, my thoughts drifted to home, my wife and children. That is when I finally and fully realized, whether I liked it or not, others had to share my secret.

"I remained relaxed almost as if it was the most natural thing in the world, but also I felt like a liar, living a false existence, doing things which were less than natural to me as I practised my deception on both myself and my family. I thought that this is absolutely ridiculous and I can't go through the rest of my life living a life which increasingly looked like one big lie after another," said Jack.

"When you said 'doing things which were less than natural,' what exactly were you thinking of? Was it your present male existence or the process of relaxing with your female self?"

"I was referring to my need to live in a pressure cooker as I strived to protect both myself and my firm in our commercial activities. At that time I saw the process of crossdressing as being perfectly natural and something to be greatly desired. Literally, I pined for it. Now, when I'm not under pressure and living with anxieties and stress, then the picture changes and I view my masculine activities as being desirable and natural. The crossdressing process and strong desire to be a woman remain, but they seem less desirable and become something that can be placed on the back burner. However, it seldom ceases to appear natural. It's a comfort to know I can lean back on it when I'm anxious and stressed out."

"When this occurs do you feel that you're finding comfort in the fantasy, or do you feel it goes deeper than that?" asked Dr. Myers.

"Well, of course, there is obviously an element of fantasy, but it isn't erotic. When fantasizing there seems to be a clear element of escaping from the unpleasant realities of the moment. As to whether it goes deeper than that, I have to say that I believe it does. You see, I'm fully appreciative of all the disadvantages of being a woman; sometimes a second class citizen in our society, a receiver of put downs, harassments, a person tied to her duties as a mother and homemaker, sometimes a breadwinner, a lack of independence in many matters, and a host of other considerations which I'm sure are very real.

"I'm sure also that some transsexuals get carried away with the glamour, the gloss and all the other attractive accoutrements of what we sometimes see as being part of the womanly role, even if in real life few woman really achieve this idyllic dream.

"Knowing all this I have to ask myself why I always knew that I should have been female and want to be female now. I can only describe it as being a comfort in the mind and it overrides all the negative factors I've mentioned. In fact, it buoys me up when I would be otherwise depressed and feeling a sense of worthlessness. It sort of offsets those periods when a lack of self-esteem can pull you down. It's like a tug-of-war between the male reality, which I see as I stand before the mirror or go to the toilet and hear when I speak, and the female presence within which wants expression, but can't get out. Before I gained an understanding of it and the problem started to become manageable, there were times when the experience seemed to tear me apart," Jack replied.

"Very well put," said the doctor. "What you have just expressed is the genesis of gender dysphoria. It's something which many well-meaning people simply can't understand no matter how they try. Every complaint, condition or disease starts with something of a specific nature, a breakdown in muscle quality, a wearing away of bones or organs, an infection by virus or bacteria, it might even be a genetic deficiency about which more seems to be coming to light with frequent new discoveries.

"The strange thing about your condition of transsexualism is, now it's generally agreed by those with expertise in this field, that its origins are to be found sometime in the first trimester of pregnancy. It appears to be started by a hormonal imbalance which in turn may originate from a genetic deficiency. The genetic aspects are very suppositional at the moment, but I personally believe that research is gradually pointing in this direction. We can't witness the process of either hormonal or genetic factors in the creation of the human fetus because we only get to know of their effects after the event, by which time the evidence of their role as creative forces have been obliterated by the process of growing up. We know the roles of hormones in sustaining masculinity in a male and femininity in a female, but all that comes after the initial events which start the human fetus and cause us to develop as one sex or the other.

"By the way, I should mention the Rakewood case again. As you know from the news reports, David was a patient of mine and what I'm going to say may go beyond the evidence of the inquest. I appreciate that this gave you a big shock. As you have pointed out there were many similarities between your situation and his, even down to the fairly similar standings in local society. There are obviously details which are and must remain confidential, but let me reassure you that the domestic arrangements and David's heavy drinking habit were vastly different from yours. You seem determined to face your problem head on and will do so without the aid of the bottle, and there's no indication that your wife is a wholly unreasonable woman. Don't let someone else's misfortune dwell on your mind, Jack, as I have a feeling that the outcome is going to be a lot better and a good deal different in your case."

The interview concluded with Jack firmly resolved that at the very first opportunity he had to discuss his problem with Moira. As doctor and patient parted company Dr. Myers final words were, "And don't forget, Jack, we are only as far away as the telephone if either of you need help or advice."

* * * * *

As usual Jack and Moira were concerned to hear of any progress with Jeremy. The day after the last appointment with Dr. Myers, Jack had lunch with Captain Steve Jones at a quality downtown hotel where there was no danger of running into Jeremy.

"I've been keeping an eye on the lad every few days. He's not hard to find around Main and Hastings. Once I accosted him in a lane shooting up in the doorway to a warehouse. He didn't see me approaching him and only became aware of me when he could see my boots and trousers at his eye level. He looked at me and nearly jumped out of his skin.

"Oh fuck, what the hell are you doing here. I guess you've been hired by Dad to spy on me." said Jeremy.

"No lad," I said. "I've got better things to do, but for sure I expect to come down a lane like this one of these days in the next few months and find you dead. Dead from being beaten up, dead from a knifing or dead from an overdose. Where the hell are your brains, Jeremy? Is this what you want, death on the installment plan at the end of a needle?" I asked him.

"Aw, piss off, you old fart. I'm not interested. If you don't watch it you're the one who is going to get knifed and then it'll be me finding you dead in a back alley," Steve quoted Jeremy.

"Just then I noticed a shadowy figure out of the corner of my eye. It was someone stealthily approaching me. I turned and saw he was carrying a knife. I grabbed his arm and swung him over my shoulder. He fell and dropped the knife, but better still I snapped his arm and he was writhing in pain."

"I called 911 on my mobile for ambulance and the police patrol. I made Jeremy sit where he was and then laid a complaint against the other guy. The guy was taken to a first aid station to get his arm fixed and the police officer put the knife in a plastic bag and placed Jeremy in the back of the car after cuffing him. I had already been able to check with my friend at the station and found that this was the first time that Jeremy had been taken in, so it probably came as a shock to him."

"What will they do to him," asked Jack, his voice betraying a little alarm.

"Probably very little, maybe if he's lucky they'll hold him long enough to dry out of his drug habit. On the other hand if they feel that there was some collusion between Jeremy and the guy who attacked me, maybe longer. Perhaps a charge of aiding in an assault, but even that would probably not draw more than ninety days in the local cooler," answered Steve Jones.

"That's not very good," said Jack contemplatively.

"I agree, but there's lots worse that could happen to him. If they keep him inside for ninety days, there's an excellent chance that he will, despite agonizing withdrawal pains, come out having kicked the habit although he'll be very fragile. If we can get to him at that moment of discharge and whisk him away before the drug pushers get to him, there is a some chance for him."

"Steve, you know we met through Doctor Fellowes who spoke highly of your qualifications for dealing with addicts. I've no problem with what you are doing with Jeremy and I know it has to be a matter of tough love. For me as a parent I know I'll not get through to him by any form of sweet reason, but knowing you've had an addiction yourself why do you suppose kids like Jeremy go off the rails. He's not been treated any differently than his sister or brother and no one has had any advantage over the other?" asked Jack.

Steve thought for a moment. "Some people seem to have naturally addictive personalities for no doubt many reasons. My addiction was caused I think by loneliness at sea particularly when

I reached captain. I nearly lost a ship due to negligence caused by drinking on the job and had my certificate suspended for a year. I put her ashore in the Sulu Sea and while they got her off, the bottom damage was very bad. After that I never went deep sea again preferring to stay closer to home on the B.C. coast.

"As to why Jeremy is affected and the others aren't I can only guess. There may be something inside which he is trying to deal with. You know the Teachers Federation estimates that about 50 per cent of all teenage suicides are kids trying to cope with homosexuality or even sometimes transsexuality, but coming up against unsympathetic parents they take what they think is the best way out and kill themselves.

"It's possible that Jeremy is trying to cope in his own way by drowning out something that is deeply troubling to him. They simply choke on their problem like one client who spent twelve years off and on in mental institutions. Nothing on God's Green Earth would get him to talk about his hidden transsexual condition, instead he took to alcohol which was killing him. By accident one of his parents discovered evidence that he might be transsexual. When confronted he admitted he was, and from then on proper treatment could start and his alcoholism was eliminated. Substitute heroin for alcohol but I can only hazard a guess as to what's bothering with Jeremy and I could be miles off. We just have to be watchful for any clue," concluded Captain Jones.

Jack heard these remarks as his mind drifted into another area with Jeremy. Could transsexuality be the hidden problem that his son was wrestling with? He knew the condition was not usually regarded as being hereditary, but nonetheless he made a mental note to discuss this possibility with Dr. Myers.

* * * * *

Simon Guthrie and his wife Peggy were personal friends of the Dempsters. The Guthries also knew the Rakewoods as friends and for Simon, David Rakewood and his firm had been important legal clients. Now that the Rakewood estate was being wound up, one of Simon Guthrie's duties was to look after the relevant legal matters. This included the sale of Rakewood Fabricators Ltd. as his widow did not think she was capable of running it. This was one of her wisest decisions in a personal history which had been notable for its lack of wisdom.

Guthrie needed some professional engineering advice regarding the equipment and capabilities of the fabrication plant and naturally turned to Jack Dempster. On this occasion they had a four o'clock appointment at Dempster's office.

"We have a potential buyer for the Rakewood plant, but he's making it subject to an independent professional engineer's survey. If you or your firm can handle that, I think we can close this deal and, confidentially, put several millions into Mrs. Rakewood's purse," said Guthrie.

"That should look after her and her children's needs pretty well," responded Jack.

"She'll be okay, without a doubt," Simon said. "They have that huge house on Sunset Drive. It was always much bigger than what they needed and, with him gone, the place must seem very empty. She stayed with us after the inquest for about five days and told us that our little four-bedroom place was plenty big enough for her family. I think she'll sell Sunset Drive and buy a more modest and sensible place."

As the conversation veered from business matters to more personal issues, Jack was hoping that Simon would say something about Rakewood's transsexualism. He didn't have long to wait.

"That was a tragic business," volunteered Simon. "When I went through his diary after the coroner returned it to me with his other private papers, I was struck with how beautifully David could express his problems in writing. There was no doubt that he'd known he was really transsexual for most of his life. But it could also be seen from his writing just how desperately afraid he was that anyone would ever find out about his guilty secret. The only person who ever knew, aside from his psychiatrist, was this Sylvia Leighton, the call girl who was called as a witness -- very willingly on her part, I might add. Sylvia was actually the first person he met who understood the true nature of his problem. I met her twice and found that she was quite a pleasant person who had been very kind to David. He was happy to pay her generously.

"But, y'know, that's a helluva comment on his opinion of his own circle. He evaluated us all and came to the conclusion he could rely on none of us for a fair judgement, some understanding, some humanity and compassion. Ron Simpson, whom you know, was also one of his close friends, as indeed he's one of mine. After all the details came out, he didn't know whether to feel insulted or humiliated that Dave had not seen fit to take him into his confidence," Simon added.

Jack listened intently and felt that this might be a good time to break his own news to someone whom he felt would have an intelligent, well-balanced understanding. As the moment drew closer he could hear his heart pounding, but here was the opportunity he needed.

"Simon," said Jack in a trembling voice. "I have something to tell you which no doubt will shock you, but for God's sakes I have to tell someone beyond my psychiatrist."

Simon Guthrie looked at his friend and could see he was literally shaking. "What is it, Jack?" he asked gently.

"I'm transsexual too."

For a moment Guthrie looked like he had been struck across the face, so surprised was he by this unlikely piece of news.

"Oh, my God! You poor, poor bugger! You could knock me over with a feather. What a surprise that I could have two friends who are transsexual. Jack, do you feel like a drink? I know I need one! Let's walk over to the club and find a quiet corner and then you can tell me all about it."

"That's a good idea, " said Jack, relieved at the prospect of relaxing a little as he told Simon of his problems.

At the club Simon opened his locker and pulled out bottles of rye and Scotch whisky. "Will these suit your pleasure, Jack, or would you fancy something else?"

"They're perfectly fine," replied Jack, who was not much of a drinker.

"Okay, carry on from where we left off at your office. You say you're transsexual. Are you doing anything about it?" asked Simon matter of factly.

"Yes, I'm consulting the psychiatrist who attended David Rakewood. She's Doctor Margaret Myers and I find her excellent."

"Have you told anyone else yet? Like your wife maybe."

"No, you're the first, except for the doctor and her partner, Doctor Fellowes," replied Jack. Now that he was talking he had calmed down and was feeling relieved that he could get it out. He told Simon everything he could think of, particularly the events of the past few months.

"Did you have any idea of Rakewood's problem?" asked Simon.

"No, not even a hint of it and I guess the same would apply in his view of me," replied Jack.

"Yes, I understand that secrecy and self-repression are two of the worst aspects of transsexualism. You can't get it out a little at a time. When it comes out, it comes in a rush and that in turn gives people the biggest shock of their lives. Unfortunately Dave never had the courage to tell anyone, except Sylvia, the witness. He was afraid of rejection and ridicule and being ostracized by everyone. There's no question he was right in his assessment of some people, but he would have found a good many who would have accepted his explanation and become supportive, had he faced the truth. It's no use condemning after the event, but for my part I wouldn't have condemned then and I don't condemn him now. Nor do I condemn you, Jack. I'm glad you mentioned it to me. That way I might be able to help, but if one doesn't know, how can one ever help?" asked Simon.

"That's true. I guess honesty is a critical factor. But it still sends chills through me when I think of all the people I have to deal with," replied Jack.

"It's the only way to handle it, I'm afraid. Because you told me quite openly, you've earned my respect. You have as much right to a healthy and happy life as anyone else and if this is what it takes, so be it. I'll do anything I can to help you, Jack, but how does Moira stand in all this?"

"I have to tell her. She has to know and the sooner the better. I think once I get that confrontation behind me I can handle any others. Moira is really the key to a successful change, which in my view includes holding our family together. If she supports me, I think the rest of the family will fall into line. If she turns against me, I think it will then become very tough indeed. And then there's Jeremy, of course. He's a special case who needs any sheet anchor he can find if he is ever to break out of his addiction. I have a lot of difficulty in knowing how to deal with that situation when he has a father who wants to be a woman.

"Knowing that Moira is so concerned over what she sees as a deterioration in my health," Jack continued glumly. "I feel so totally dishonest in not having told her. Moira is a wonderful wife and mother, whom I love dearly, but I think this fear of dealing with her is one of the reasons for my underlying anxiety."

Simon considered his glass for a moment. "I suppose you feel as though you'll be doing something dastardly, like plunging a knife in her back. I don't suppose the image of Kathy Rakewood has helped any either."

"Yeah, that's the truth, all right," replied Jack.

"Knowing Moira, I don't think you'll have a repeat of the Rakewood situation. Moira is much too sensible for that. Oh, I'm not suggesting it'll be easy and the initial shock might be very disconcerting for both of you. She'll receive advice from her father, Professor Lyle Davidson, one of the great gentlemen of the law, at whose knee I gained much of my legal education. There's much of old Lyle in Moira and don't forget she also has a law degree which she didn't earn by being a fool. She'll think before she puts her foot in her mouth. In any event she has to be told and I would agree the sooner the better. I'll be happy to talk to her, after you've made a clean breast of it. For me to speak to her now on your behalf would only mean that you're putting off what you have to do and that is to deal with this thing directly as husband and wife."

"Yes, you're right, I know and I wouldn't presume on you doing anything for me until after she knows. I have to face the music alone and risk a helluva lot. But, it's a risk that's unavoidable. Better that than having my health deteriorate as it has to a surprising degree. Little that is specific as yet. It's what's commonly called 'being badly run down' which is just the kind of thing that sooner or later leads to complications, heart, high blood pressure, digestive problems and so on. I already have a hiatus hernia and it's a barometer of how I feel. For example, I can't handle more than two weak whiskies, well cut with soda water, otherwise I'll pay for it tonight, not by getting drunk, but just in discomfort until I drown it in a prescription drug," responded Jack.

"What about your firm, Jack? How do you suppose old John Haliburton will react?" asked Simon.

"That's a helluva good question. Because of his looks and gruff but kindly manner, he's known around the office as Spencer Tracey. His life has been a good one, but his favourite daughter is a lesbian. Handling that one has taught him the meaning of tolerance. He told me about this some four of five years ago. Needless to say he hoped to see her married and give his wife and himself more grandchildren. He said, 'What d'you do, Jack? Throw her out or let her bring her girlfriend home?' Shirley and he evidently stewed over all this and concluded that it was better to welcome the girlfriend than to lose a daughter. Now he says the whole family welcomes the two of them. The girlfriend is evidently a very nice person. So I suppose you could say that John has learned a lesson in tolerance."

By now a couple of hours had passed. "Why don't you and I have dinner tonight in the dining room. I'll phone Peggy and tell her not to wait. I guess you'd better do the same with Moira."

Jack went to the bank of phones in the hallway. "Hi, honey. Simon Guthrie has been consulting me on some matters to do with the Rakewood estate. We're at the Pacific Club and he has asked me to stay here for supper. Sorry it's such short notice, but it's important. I'll be home maybe at nine or as soon as I can."

"Okay dear, I forgive you. It's only a stew and it'll keep," replied Moira. Jack was always home for dinner at a reasonable hour, so she knew it must be something important that would keep him away.

Over dinner, Simon revealed that he had a surprising familiarity with transsexualism. "One of our women lawyers handled the case of *Landry v. Landry*[*], one of the celebrated law cases of the past year. Mrs. Landry was suing for divorce, claiming her husband's transsexualism as the cause of a complete marital breakdown. The truth was that Mrs. Landry wanted to make a public spectacle of it all in order to punish her husband.

"The judge wondered why, in view of the medical evidence, she insisted on dragging it through the courts. A few more months of living apart would have created grounds of non-cohabitation and a simple dissolution of the marriage and a workable division of assets and liabilities. The judge said that transsexualism was

* The case of Landry v. Landry is entirely fictitious.

of itself not a ground for a divorce. That would be like divorcing someone who had contracted cancer because of the cancer. What the judge said was that the social stigma was more relevant. The wife would not consider the husband's dilemma for what it was – a definable medical condition. She wanted to turn it into something indecent by way of a public hanging, so to speak.

"The judge recognized that an irreversible breakdown in the marriage had occurred and granted the divorce, although he made it clear to Mrs. Landry that he wasn't going to give her, her pound of flesh as well. He said transsexualism is a natural but abnormal condition and to blame her husband for that was unreasonable. He had no more say in his condition than the fact he had been born with blue eyes rather than brown. I understand he's successfully completed surgery and his transition since. She is now a happy woman. I hear Mrs. Landry has a new man in her life, so I hope she's happy too," Simon said.

"I guess that's what David Rakewood was afraid of, a public hanging type of thing," Jack responded. "I don't think that's the way Moira will react no matter how badly let down she might feel. You can see certain things in a person's character. Moira just doesn't have the venom that Kathy obviously has, so I'll have to hope for the best. Before we go I want to thank you, Simon, for being so understanding. I feel three times more confident than I did before I spoke to you. Just knowing people are capable of listening and understanding is an immense step forward," said Jack, as the two friends shook hands and parted.

Chapter Seven

The Spanish Beauty

Since seeing Dr. Myers, Jack's courage had evaporated to the point where he was questioning the wisdom once again of letting matters go any further. Should he or shouldn't he? On this basis he could continue to procrastinate forever, but the more he procrastinated the more his conscience bothered him. Was he facing up to the realities of his situation? No, of course he wasn't. The more he procrastinated the more he swung from the fantasy dreams of a life he craved, to the horrible possibilities of reality.

Through Dr. Myers, Jack came to know and became friendly with a younger attractive woman who had been a man. Linda Bowker worked only a few blocks away as an insurance underwriter and he would meet her occasionally for lunch. She had always been employed with the one company since she started work. When the time came for her surgery she was readily granted a leave of absence for a couple of months during the most critical period of her transition. This was part of her routine for reorganizing her life during the period when she had started to live as a woman until she had affected her full gender change.

Jack was curious over lunch one day. "What happened in your life, Linda, to make you pursue your gender change?"

Linda frowned slightly as she framed her reply. "I guess I was really quite an effeminate young boy. I was an only child, with a mother who doted on me and a father who by being tolerant, really could care less about me being brought up in the masculine image. It was assumed, I suppose, that I was developing as a gay and I can hardly blame anyone for that. I regarded myself as gay, but there was one key factor which was out of character."

"Oh, what was that, if you'll pardon me being curious?" said Jack very quietly.

"Well, I moved into the gay community and being quite an attractive, but effeminate teenager, I had the attention of a flock of gay men who saw me as their target. Yes, I slept around with them, but I found it didn't really work for me. The men I was attracted to were all heterosexual and, needless to say, they in turn were not turned on by me. How could they be? I was still obviously a male of a type that hetero men found repugnant."

"Truly a Catch-22 situation then," suggested Jack.

"Yes, it really was. Also, because I had a good career ahead of me in insurance I never wanted to risk that through any indiscretion," replied Linda.

"What made you choose insurance?" asked Jack.

"We're an insurance family. Dad worked in insurance and then, when I was still quite young, he set up his own business as an independent insurance broker and agent. His firm is S.B. Bowker & Company and, until very recently, he was president of the Insurance Brokers Association. He has quite a prominent status in the industry. My mother was a secretary in the office he was in before he set up his own business. When that happened she became his partner not only in marriage, but in the business. On the whole it has worked well for them."

"What happened when you wanted to choose a career?" asked Jack

"Well, I guess that was the first time they confronted the reality of my supposedly gay personality. Whether they were uncomfortable with it at the time is hard to say. They encouraged me to go into the Northern Canada Insurance Company, which I did. Very conveniently Dad had a large account with the company which gave me some leverage. I gained professional qualifications with the highest marks in Canada in my final year, so I was looked upon as something of a genius.

"That wouldn't do any harm, I'm sure," remarked Jack.

"That's right and it was after that I decided to see Dr. Myers. She helped me get sorted out. Although I had a clear view ahead on my career, nothing but confusion reigned in my mind over my sexuality. In the end I had surgery about five years ago and have never regretted it. I made a big effort to convert everything. I took dancing and deportment lessons, studied as a model, in fact, I did everything to create an entirely new me," replied Linda, as she pulled a photo of her old self out of her wallet.

"You certainly did a fantastic job, Linda," said Jack as he looked at the back of the photo. "So your former name was Leslie, eh! What does the future hold for you now?"

"Career-wise, I'm talking to my parents about entering the family business and eventually I plan to take it over from them. That I would like. I was able to change on the job at Northern Canada because I was very much in a backroom position, not meeting the public. I don't think I could have done it too easily while working behind the counter in an insurance brokerage office. I think that is one thing my parents had on their minds when I told them.

As far as my sex life is concerned, it's fine. I have heterosexual boy friends who know of my past and it doesn't stop them from wanting my body. So far no one has wanted it badly enough to want a permanent relationship. I have to face the facts. Maybe they never will because with the best will in the world there probably remains a tiny lingering prejudice against even the best of transsexuals. If a heterosexual man has a choice it's inevitable it seems to me, that his own biology will dictate that he wants a biological woman. I'm quite philosophical about it and I've made up my mind to enjoy my life to the fullest as I strive for my own financial independence," said Linda.

"I don't quite know what my view of men will become following a change. At the moment I feel quite unable to speculate on the subject," responded Jack.

"I don't think I'd concern myself about that question at this point. That one will unfold naturally over time. When you go through this so-called sex-change, you're emerging in a new version of yourself. Many find this idea repugnant as they claim you're tampering with nature and going against God's intentions. That may be so if you subscribe to heavy religious ideas. But in all logic it is acceptable for a woman to have breast implants, a man to shave everyday, any person to have a deformity fixed by plastic surgery. Anyone can dye their hair a colour different from the one allocated to us by nature. There are a thousand and one other things to improve our view of ourselves. If that's so, what's wrong with an effort to improve our mental well-being, to increase our confidence and so on. If it takes a transsexual operation to blow away the cobwebs in one's mind and allow a person to live happily and healthily within him or herself, instead of constantly fretting, getting stressed out and overly anxious, none of which are healthy in the long term, then I say go with it. That's justification enough."

"I see you wear a full face of make-up. Is that because you have to, or is it because you want to?" asked Jack who found Linda to be quite fascinating. She was so straight to the point in addressing the issues. If she had ever had any inhibitions she clearly had freed herself of them.

"You can condemn make-up as a deception. I'm wearing make-up right now because it makes me feel better about myself. I'm not sending a message to all the men I come into contact with that I'm ready and available to lay with them. The answer to that lies in my own moral values. Sure I've slept with men, but it is not for a mere sexual sensation. I have to like a man, there has to be some feeling of mutuality, that we're together because we both want to be together. Any man who thinks he can have me for my body alone is suffering from delusions," Linda paused to gather her thoughts.

"Keep in mind that there's no universal answer. The question that all transsexuals have to grapple with, is, why me? Why has nature or the creator singled me out for special attention? Why did nature at the point of conception decree that I should be born male rather than female? Why, having decreed that I should be male do I have a lifelong uncomfortable idea that God made His mistake in the way He did? These questions are unanswerable in any proven way. The only answers are to be found in our own philosophy. There are many drawbacks to being a woman, but in the end I can say to myself in every way, with satisfaction, that I'm glad I clarified my womanhood. In my mind I always was a woman in a man's body. Although I looked like a man when I was one, I, and I alone, could see, could feel and could sense almost every aspect of being a woman. That, in my view, is what distinguishes transsexualism from every other condition known to mankind. We are truly unique."

"That's the best description I've ever heard of transsexualism," Jack said. "It demonstrates why even the best professional practitioner can never quite finally put the last few building blocks in place. You have to do that yourself. The professionals can never tell you what to do because everything you do, has to be your own decision. To fully understand transsexualism I believe you have to have lived the experience."

"I'd say you've got it exactly," replied Linda.

There was a pause while the waitress refilled their cups. "You seem to have handled things very well. Just one thing, how did the insurance company you work for handle the matter?" asked Jack.

"Oh, it was like putting the cat among the pigeons at first. It caused consternation right through to head office in

Toronto. They knew what transsexualism was, or so they thought, but they'd never been confronted by it in an employee. My manager was sympathetic and supportive to the extent that he could be, but management in Toronto wanted to do a sort of forensic study on the entire subject which I suppose was reasonable in the circumstances. They asked Dr. Myers for a complete assessment, which she gave them, but I think a strong card was played when my parents got into the act.

"My mother had said privately that she would prefer a heterosexual daughter to a gay son. Now that I've made this adjustment, I am truly heterosexual now and I enjoy heterosexual men. I am out of the gay scene totally and for straight people this is very important.

"The company moderated its concern when my parents came in and told them that they wanted me to go through with this and become their daughter. They didn't challenge that statement for any reason I could see and none was given. Doug Melnick, the branch manager, assured the senior management that I wouldn't be dealing with the public except on the phone while I was going through the transition. They were concerned about the toilets, but Doug polled the female staff who said they had no problem provided I was fully dressed and presented as a female. After all, when you go into a toilet cubicle to deal with nature's needs, who's there to examine your genitals? In turn, I assured him that once I showed up as Linda I would never revert to Leslie, who would then be a part of my past. On the whole it has worked okay. There were a few insults and innuendoes, but I was able to handle them or ignore them and the excitement quickly died down," replied Linda.

"Let's change the subject Jack and talk about you, while we are exchanging confidences. For instance how do you know, if you'll like being a woman with all the messing about with hair, make up and clothes which women undertake on a daily basis?" asked Linda.

"Well, I suppose I don't know for sure, although I'm very comforted in my mind when I fantasize about it. I have never been a cross-dresser like a transvestite. I have experimented a little in secret with my wife's stuff and purchased a few articles of my own, including a dress, but the experience while pleasant enough becomes very unsettling afterwards and just makes me envious of what should've been," replied Jack.

Linda had been an experienced cross-dresser long before she went for surgery. "Aside from the fact that you have to face your wife on it all, and that's something I can't help you with, you should try cross-dressing occasionally and go out in public. In your social position I realize that you have to take great care as to the neighbourhood you would frequent for an experiment, but for what it's worth you'd likely be safer in the gay neighbourhoods of the city. Even then you might be surprised at who you might run into and who is supposedly straight but is cheating on his wife."

"Would you be able to help me, Linda?" Jack asked a little anxiously. "I've done a little cross-dressing, but I simply don't know my way around these problems. It's always been in secret and no one alive has ever seen me."

"Yes, I could. What you should do is come around to my apartment. We're about the same size and height and I could show you how to apply make-up to the best effect. I'll lend you some necessary clothing items to get you started. I suggest you have a go at this a few times before you come out into the open with your wife. If you can't carry it off, meaning probably a lack of confidence, it would be grim if your wife totally rejected you. You're not a bad-looking guy and I think you will make a passable woman. If you don't try it no one will ever know, least of all yourself."

Arrangements were made for the two to meet at Linda's apartment. Jack felt a surge of emotions as he drove over to Linda's, including suppressed excitement at times bordering on panic. He chose a weekend when Moira had travelled out of town with Josh and Jennifer to stay with relatives of hers.

He was very nervous as he rode in the elevator to Linda's apartment. She met him at the door, greeted him and offered him a drink, as she put it "to strengthen your nerves." She looked very attractive although dressed informally. Her blonde hair was piled high on her head and as usual her make-up was immaculate.

After some chatter during which Jack downed his drink, she said, "Jack, do you want a shower?"

"I wouldn't think so, as I had one just before leaving the house to come over."

"Okay, take this gown and strip off in the spare bedroom. I'll bring some undies and pantyhose."

After a little rummaging around she handed Jack a new pair of black pantyhose with black panties, underslip and a bra. "Get these on, taking care to handle the hose carefully, otherwise you'll put a run in them, and then I'll decide what dress to put you into after I've done your make-up."

Jack trembled with nervous excitement so badly that his teeth seemed to be chattering. He had watched his wife pulling on her pantyhose and had done it before on several occasions so knew how to handle this. In a few minutes he was ready for the next stage in his transformation.

"When you're ready come into my bedroom and I'll do you up in front of my dressing table, but first I want to try this wig on you."

Jack's hair was almost black and he had a very pale skin, but quite a dark beard shadow. At Linda's direction he pulled on the attractive black dress with its oversize white collar and slipped his feet into black high heel pumps. She put a plastic make-up sheet around his shoulders. Then followed foundation as she used heavy base to minimize his beard shadow. She pulled the black wig on his head and teased it around until she was satisfied with the effect and then went to work on his eyes and brows. Jack watched the transformation with fascination.

"Now comes the 'piece de resistance,'" said Linda as she studied his mouth for a moment and then outlined the shape of the lips with a lipstick pencil. "Don't try to look, Jack. I want you to see yourself the first time as a complete work of art."

She finished the make-up and then rooted around for jewellery, including clip-on earrings.

"Now stand up before that full-length mirror and meet Jacqueline. You'll find the shoes a bit strange until you get used to them." Jack struggled to his feet finding the shoes a little difficult to balance in and walked over to the mirror.

What he saw stunned him. Here was the image of a handsomely striking, middle-aged woman looking back at him. She looked surprisingly slender and the black hair with her natural pale skin and the darkish red lipstick made her look rather Spanish, she thought. She was so taken aback and fascinated with what she saw, she could hardly look away from the mirror.

"Yes, that's you, Jacqueline, and you are quite a beauty who can only improve with time. Electrolysis will eventually get rid of that beard shadow and then you'll look every inch the handsome Spanish beauty."

"That's interesting that you can see the Spanish in me just as I did. I have Spanish ancestors, but Jacqueline might take a little getting used to. I guess I would get Jackie which is hardly much of a transition from Jack."

"That's true, but I think both names suit you. It's probably best to stay close to your original name and have the same initials. You'll still get Jack from some people out of force of habit, but it'll be easier for them to add the 'ie' onto it than remember to call you Melanie or Jessica or some such name." Linda said.

The two sat in Linda's living room over further drinks. Jack's body seemed to soak it all up as he learned to relax. He was pleasantly surprised with his appearance and gained greater confidence as Linda assured him that she would have no difficulty in being seen with him in public, "as you pass very well."

"You will have to wear a heavy make-up to cover your blue beard shadow, that is until you get along with electrolysis, but really the more I look at you, the more stunning I believe you'll become," added Linda.

Over a last drink Jack philosophized about his future. "I've got a great many things to consider in dealing with this. Y'see, unlike some, I happen to genuinely love my wife and three kids, although one of them is a major problem. On the surface I have an ideal domestic situation plus a good job. Really, Linda, I've everything a man could possibly want, including that male barometer --material success. Why flush it down the toilet, one could ask? I've nibbled at the fringes of the problem for years, including bad sleep habits and all the stress caused by fatigue, but that unfortunate Rakewood case simply brought it all home to me finally and irrevocably. I can't live in a vacuum in my mind any longer. It's as simple as that and everything we discussed over lunch last week has underlined the certainty of it. I know now that I have to be prepared to risk all in order to gain some peace of mind. In the next few days I'll be telling Moira. This time it can't be put off any longer."

Jack drove home late at night. The house was silent except for the two German shepherd dogs who did their duty as watchdogs as soon as they heard Jack's car come into the driveway. He had reverted to Jack before leaving Linda's apartment. After a glass of milk he went to bed laying there silently contented and knowing more than ever before, that he had to broach the subject to Moira as soon as she returned. He read for a short while, but what he saw with his eyes was not being relayed to his brain. His mind was consumed by the experience of this evening as he replayed the entire routine in his imagination. There was something very unique and beautiful as the curtain was drawn back on the emerging Jacqueline. He liked what he saw and knew that this one little event had changed his life forever. His satisfaction was tempered by his conscience. His exultancy was mixed with his regret, but the nervousness that had caused him to always vacillate had now given way to a new confidence.

That night he slept better than he had done for a long time. Tomorrow was a public holiday and it would open a new chapter in his life. "Dear God," he thought "I just pray it's a good day and that Moira and the kids will return safe and sound. Please God help them all to understand, but when the blow falls after I tell them, help me to land it softly without pulling everything down around me."

* * * * *

"He's going to go through hell for a while. Maybe a week or more" said Steve Jones as he and Jack Dempster enjoyed a brief lunch with each other.

Jeremy Dempster had been sentenced to 90 days in provincial jail for his supposed part in the attempted assault on Stephen Jones. Whether Jeremy had in fact been part of such an event Steve and Jack could only speculate. When asked by the judge for his opinion, Steve said "I doubt if there was malicious intent." The judge addressed Jeremy when he said.

"I'm going to do you a favour, Mr. Dempster. I'm sentencing you to ninety days in jail which I realize sets you up with a criminal record, but if you have any sense at all you'll see it is the beginning of a new dawn for you when you leave behind a very painful and damaging period in your life. The report before me indicates you came from a good home with responsible parents, who wish for nothing more than to see you return to good health and on your way to a successful career. I understand that you had plans to become an architect which is surely an honourable and worthwhile profession. This is your chance to get off your pathway to destruction. With this sentence I'm ordering that you be delivered to the custody of your parents when you're discharged from prison. I want to hear nothing of you returning to the street and if you should appear before me again the sentence will be far heavier next time."

Jack saw his son being led away and before he disappeared Jeremy turned and waved to his father. Jack returned the wave and felt reassured that there was hope for Jeremy, but he now wondered how both Steve and Jeremy would take the news of his forthcoming gender change. Once he had told Moira there was no doubt that the news would travel fast, first to his family and then to outsiders and there would be no need to withhold the secret any longer. Jack felt scared at the same time as he anticipated relief from all that built up internal pressure. Would Jeremy need a father figure? As befitted his role as father, it was Jack who had shouldered the main burden of dealing with this episode in Jeremy's life. Would the news of Jack's change undermine Jeremy's fragile opportunity for a normalized life? This window of opportunity would be brief enough and if it was mishandled in any way it could result in Jeremy sliding back.

Tomorrow, Moira was due to return and the cat would be let out of the bag. He just hoped that all hell would not break loose in the process.

Chapter Eight

To Tell the Honest Truth

"Oh, my God," gasped Moira as she bit her right index finger to stop from screaming out loud. Her husband, after days of agonizing, finally blurted out his secret. To say that it had all taken Moira by surprise was an understatement. She felt she had been bowled over as if caught up in a tidal wave. Whatever her suspicions about the state of Jack's health they had not included any belief that he was transsexual. Jack was sitting opposite her in their living room his eyes streaming with tears and nose running as if he had just caught a cold.

"Jack, this is horrible, like a living nightmare. I never suspected any such thing. Why didn't you tell me years ago, if you knew all along you had this condition? It's like going away for a pleasant holiday and wheeling into the driveway to find that your home containing all your possessions has burned down to a heap of ashes. At this moment I look at our marriage and see a heap of ashes. What do I do now? Sift through the debris to see if anything of our past has survived except for memories? Do I reject you outright, because my soul feels like it has been murdered? Or do I try to find a new focal point in my life and start to build afresh? God knows, I don't know at this point! I need time to think about it all. There are a million things to consider, our children, our parents, our home and a decision as to whether we two have any remaining future together," she added.

Jack had been silent after dropping his big surprise. He had had a momentary vision of himself dropping a tray load of valuable chinaware and breaking every piece. His pale face was more like the colour of white parchment. He was perspiring profusely as he mopped his brow and face with a small towel he had grabbed out of the kitchen. His stomach was in nervous knots and he knew that if this kept up he would be running to the bathroom. He was looking at Moira for any sign of a softer response on her part. She was softly sobbing, having given up her first attempt at a hard, unreconcilable attitude.

"Moira, darling, is there anything I can say to ease your pain?"

"Yes, as long as what you say doesn't do further damage," she replied.

"Can you believe me when I say that I truly love you and this is the hardest thing I've ever had to do in my life?" said Jack. "It's impossible to talk about it until some form of pressure or crisis takes over and takes it out of your hands. I had hoped I'd be able to keep it concealed until the end of my life so that my secret would pass with me to the grave. What can I add? I thought a happy marriage would be the answer. Our marriage has been a happy one, but in spite of this, the pressure has been enormous. That is why I have become a very poor sleeper. This is what lived in my mind every night and kept me awake, until things have reached the point where my health is being undermined and I'm in danger of completely cracking up."

"I don't know what to say. I'm in such a state of total shock. I can't respond to anything right now until my mind clears a little," Moira replied.

"I knew it would be a shock. In my mind, I've turned over the whole process of telling you a thousand times in the past year,"said Jack. "It's unfortunate, but there's no way of easing the shock by gradually telling a person. You have to get to the point with the truth as directly as you can. Can you half fire a gun so that the shell gently falls to the ground after the bang? You can't. I'm afraid that after pulling the trigger everything goes off full-blast and one has to take the consequences in terms of damage. In other words I had to get it out completely or not at all.

"Having told you of my dilemma, it seems that constructive moves are called for now. They won't put the broken egg back together again, but at least they may show us both a way ahead. Dr. Myers is available to explain in medical terms what this problem amounts to. If you know the 'how and why' of it all from an expert it might make understanding a good deal easier. For example, it might help you understand what motivates a transsexual, such as me, to keep his secret to himself and get married, in the hope that it would all go away and enable me to live a normal life. You know, I hope, I didn't marry you with any idea of deceiving you. I married you because I loved you then, and still do now. I believed spending the rest of my life with you was the best thing imaginable."

"But Jack, what has gone wrong, to disturb that perfectly acceptable set of motives?" asked Moira.

"I'm not certain myself," replied Jack regaining control of his reasoning practical side. "There has been no crisis between you and me and my business is creating no problems that are unusual. Yes, we have Jeremy to worry about, but in no way is he the cause of my problems which I knew something of long before he got into drugs. However, I sometimes wonder if at the heart of his problem, there isn't something similar lurking in the inner recesses of his mind. They tell me that often a transsexual is propelled into taking the final steps towards change as the result of some crisis triggering the need. I've had no crisis that I can identify unless the mounting strain of gender dysphoria is the crisis in itself. What I have had are hundreds of sleepless nights over a good many years and the cause of these is a sort of mourning or lamenting that I wasn't born in the opposite sex. My female alter ego makes her presence felt so strongly that for long periods I can't cast her out of my mind. Her presence torments me, while at other times she seems like an old friend. It's almost as if there's another person sharing my body and the female part of me is in constant battle with my male self for domination.

"I've described all this to the doctor. I think that maybe I'm going insane or at best going into a severe nervous breakdown, or just suffering from delusions, but that isn't the case. I'm not insane and I'm not suffering from a breakdown. What Dr. Myers tells me is that, when I was still a fetus in Mum's womb my brain failed to achieve a full differentiation. As a result there's a natural conflict between the two aspects, the female and male which started at that point and continues today. That is the source of the crisis in my life. On the one hand, I want to accept myself as a happy contented male, with the wife and family I love, a home which has everything and a good living from my business activities. But I'm simply unable to do so. It's this incongruity which is slowly destroying me.

"On the other hand, the enormous pressure to want to effect gender change is terribly powerful. It isn't something that I've consciously sought after. It's almost like nature has placed an egg inside me and my body now demands that I disgorge it. Although I don't see women as having a wonderful life in this society with all the obligations imposed on them by their biological features and gender, the idea, the glamour and female beauty are all a part of a delightful fantasy for me. The reality is simply horrendous, the challenges enormous, and the destruction I foresee very frightening," concluded Jack.

Moira now felt a little sorry for her husband. There was a little light seeping into her understanding which made it apparent that Jack's problem was far bigger than any passing fad or resort to erotic temptation. She remembered the occasions when he talked in his sleep with some strange references to things which would normally only interest a woman, and how he went deadly pale and had to retreat to the bathroom after reading the report of the inquest into the death of David Rakewood. She wondered if he saw it as a premonition of his own death in a similar way. She could see the misery in his eyes and hear the strain in his voice. For her part she had stopped sobbing.

"I'm going to get us both a cup of tea, Jack, and then we can start to talk a little about what we should do about all this. One thing, I'd like to talk to your psychiatrist and if it's okay with you I'll phone her tomorrow to book an appointment."

* * * * *

Dr. Myers seemed very relaxed and greeted Moira with a charming smile as she took a seat at the side of the doctor's desk.

"I'm well aware that this must be a distressing and confusing time for you, Mrs. Dempster. A bombshell like this is hardly something that anyone ever expects and when it happens it can be quite devastating. However, I'm glad you came in to see me first and didn't see a lawyer as your first step in dealing with your husband's problems and your own life, as the two are bound together. So where shall we start?"

Moira asked for a full description of the condition of transsexualism and the doctor's opinion as to how and why it had developed in Jack. This corroborated much that Jack had said and opened up some new possibilities of understanding.

The doctor outlined the key factors in identifying it and how it is normally treated. "We know how it developed in Jack, which is confirmed by his recollections of his infancy. It was as if a light flashed on in his brain when he was a very young boy which told him he was really meant to be a little girl. That conviction never left him. It's almost like a snapshot impression was burned into his memory. Many transsexuals remember this moment of revelation down to the tiniest detail, as indeed does Jack.

"What actually happens in the womb is not known with certainty except that it's clear that a hormone imbalance of some sort does occur and this affects the differentiation between the female and male parts of the brain which we all have. Nature provides for a full, normal differentiation, but this doesn't appear to happen in a transsexual. We know with relative certainty that this failure to differentiate is what happens. What we don't know is just why or how it happens because, by the time we become aware of gender dysphoria, even in a young child, the triggering action in the womb has long since passed."

"Could any of my children be suffering from the same thing?"

"If they are, it is not because of anything hereditary that we know of. There is less than nothing to indicate otherwise. If one of your children was affected by the condition, it would be as the result of an independent event in the child's formation. Mind you, there are recorded cases of such events among sibling brothers, which might indicate that certain aspects of procreation between the parents might be repetitive. On the other hand, the influence of one sibling, say an older brother on a younger, cannot be overlooked. When that happens I believe that the fundamentals of transsexualism must also be in place. Otherwise, such influence would not be a factor."

"I was wondering about our son, Jeremy. Could he be burdened in the same way with a case of transsexuality and his way of burying it is to resort to drugs?" asked Moira.

"You can rule out nothing, but on the law of averages I'd say it's a very remote possibility on hereditary grounds. On the other hand substance abuse is fairly common among transsexuals until they get a grip on themselves and recognise that they are only hurting themselves by placing a roadblock in their journey to dealing with their central gender identity disorder," replied Dr. Myers.

"I've noticed that Jack seems to have an instinct more like a mother in his concern for Jeremy. I've motherly concerns too but I have a slightly different view to Jack. I think I'm more pragmatic, which may also make me appear to be less sensitive to our son's predicament. I think Jeremy will come out of this, if he survives, only when he thinks he wants out of it. Jack seems to take his concerns more deeply to heart and I think this has a lot to do with his lack of sleep. What do you think?" asked Moira.

"I think there is a place for both sets of emotions, although it takes more than just "wanting" to break clear of drugs. He is not likely to do it to please his parents. He is more likely to deal with it when he sees for himself that there is something else out there in life which makes things look a whole lot better."

"Like what for example?"

"Well, one thing that's conceivable is that he might fall in love with someone who comes to him with a role model that he can see himself fitting into. It's hard to vizualise as things stand and falling in love, while natural also tends to blind us to certain aspects of the practical side of life. So also might it show him something that he never thought possible before in his drug-crazed view of life," answered the doctor.

Moira reflected on this for a moment. "You know I never would have seen it that way, but it might be a possibility. I'll pray to God that it might just happen. But for how long have you been aware of Jack's condition, Doctor?"

The doctor consulted her file. "He came to me about a year ago."

"Was he ill or something?" asked Moira.

"He wasn't ill in the conventional sense, but he was obviously fairly heavily stressed and I prescribed something to calm him down. The danger was that the problem in his mind might have led to other problems such as high blood pressure, ulcers or heart trouble. Generally he's in good physical health, but too much of this sort of pressure can easily undermine the positive features in a person's health."

"I wonder why he never mentioned this before? I wasn't even aware he was on any sort of medication."

"Secrecy and a hope that the problem will go away are two features of being an average transsexual. The secrecy results in severe repression and that can be almost like another psychological illness. The other feature 'hoping it will go away,' is an illusion. It won't go away. It may retract. It may lose its intensity, but the chances are that by some sort of process of regeneration, it will come back again often with renewed or even greater intensity. This summerizes the influences which go to make up Jack's problem.

"He wanted to share his secret with you and gradually came around to dealing with this after counselling with me. He knew he could only hope to ever deal with it if he was honest, first with himself, and then with you and others in his life. As long as he was hoping it would go away he was running away from the facts and therefore couldn't be completely honest with himself.

"A feature of all this is that it takes a long time, a lot of self-reasoning and, finally, a lot of courage to let the genie out of the bottle and come clean," the doctor continued. "I know that Jack went through a living hell while he fretted over what he eventually came to feel was unavoidable. It had to come out, even if it hurt the feelings of those he loves most. But better that than slowly being crushed under the influence of a colossal lie, as Jack saw it."

"I'm beginning to see how Jack was trapped by an awful dilemma and I feel very sorry for him," Moira said. "I can see now why he went deathly pale and had to retreat to the bathroom when he read about David Rakewood's suicide case. I think he thought he was reading his own death notice. How can I help him through this? Can you make any suggestions?"

"Yes, of course. More will gradually filter out from him as the spilt milk is mopped up, so to speak. Has he told you anything of secret crossdressing? Can you stand the thought of seeing him crossdressed? Don't be shocked too much would be my advice and try to keep an open mind. I happen to be satisfied that there has been little or no crossdressing activity until very recently. He discussed it with me beforehand and I advised him to try it, to at least see if he could stand the look of himself as a potential woman if he was determined that this was what he had to do."

The doctor glanced at Moira. She sensed that she momentarily seemed to bridle at the thought that the doctor was encouraging rather than deterring such a thing.

"I know what you're thinking. No, I wasn't pushing him into it or anything else, but he had to experiment in a controlled way. My purpose is to help him keep all four wheels on the road, so to speak. It's when transsexuals don't know where they're going or why, when they do impetuous, unwise things and get into real trouble. He has formed a friendship with another former transsexual patient of mine, a nice young woman named Linda who is in the insurance business as an underwriter. She trained as a model and has been through courses of dressing, deportment, make up and all the things a model has to know, but she's never worked as one, staying with her job in insurance. Linda dressed Jack up one night and showed me a few photos she had taken in the apartment on that one occasion when they did get together. That was about a week before he told you. Showing me the photos was with Jack's full knowledge and consent. I have not got them here, but I'm sure you'll be as agreeably surprised as I was if you see him. He looks surprisingly good. There's a touch of Spanish beauty of which Linda obviously knew how to take advantage."

For a moment Moira relaxed and smiled gently. "I've difficulty in imagining Jack successfully passing as a woman, as I've never detected any particularly feminine or effeminate traces in him."

"That isn't unusual. Effeminacy for many is an acquired or cultivated trait. To be feminine, or masculine in normal women and men is the most natural thing in the world. If Jack goes through with this he will go from being Mr. Average nice-guy to Ms. Average nice-gal."

Moira talked about their three children, Jeremy, Jennifer and Joshua. "They worry me quite a lot. They're all bright kids, although there's a huge problem at present with Jeremy as you know."

"Yes, I know about Jeremy and I think my colleague Dr. Fellowes might be able to help there, when the time is ripe." interposed Dr. Myers, "But please go on."

"I know Jack thinks the world of them as I do. I know it's a matter of the greatest concern to him as to how they'll take and handle the news. He doesn't want to see his relationship with them destroyed anymore than his relationship with me. I know he feels that it'll be as big a crisis in dealing with them as it was with me. Can you suggest anything, doctor?"

"Yes, I can. This is the point when a united front becomes most important. If you go before them like daggers opposed, you'll force them to take sides in all likelihood and in either case it may not be to your liking. There is much truth in the old idea of 'mother's sons and father's daughters'. I know he has been a good father, there will be much tugging at the paternal heart strings, and vice versa.

"On the other hand if you go before them holding hands, so to speak, you'll be sending out a clear message which spells unity. You may not like the idea of proclaiming your unity of thought and action with Jack, but think of the alternatives. A lack of unity will proclaim a schism and there are few things worse than a family divided. This, in turn, will spread to the relatives and maybe also to his job situation. No one wants to see two people sandbagging each other to death. The ordinary instinct of decent people is to lend support when they can see that a couple is working together like a well coordinated team to solve their problems.

"If a couple is perceived as being in conflict, those who might feel obliged to take sides, like your children, might feel drawn into it because they feel they have no alternative. Your friends and others, like his partners at the firm who need not be involved, might think they should remain neutral, which is usually wise. However, neutrality can take strange forms, like washing their hands of both of you. At this point the two of you might feel the world has abandoned you. Breakups are destructive at any time, but this type involving sexual issues of the most mysterious kind are probably the very worst," said Dr. Myers.

"I suppose," Moira said," at this point I feel as though I'm the one called upon to make the sacrifice in the interest of whatever stability can be maintained. I can see that in many ways I become the core of the family. I have the power to wreck everything, including his and my children's lives. I suppose the whole process of change will take a couple of years. I guess it's a short enough period in a person's lifetime to preside over an event like this. But reassure me on one thing. What is the nature of Jack's relationship with this transsexual friend? If there was a romantic relationship there, that's the one thing I could never forgive."

"I believe you can rest assured on that, Mrs. Dempster. Linda's problems were complex, but they have been resolved and they don't include a man facing possible gender reassignment. I'm completely confident of Jack's loyalty to you and the children. Everything he says and does is focused on that single factor.

"The problem for him is that he has to establish friendships with people who understand his problem and, as is so often stated, no one knows a transsexual like another transsexual. At the gender dysphoria clinic, for example, this is well understood. They make a definite effort to bring people in similar circumstances together with the idea that in mingling, people will find friendships. This can bring mutual benefits to both parties. No, I know Linda to be completely reliable. She keeps in touch with and helps others in a positive way. That's part of her mission in life."

The meeting concluded with Dr. Myers offering advice."You should stay calm and cool and let matters unfold naturally, now that they are out in the open. Don't pressure him. Now that there are no secrets between the two of you, you can discuss and plan your future moves together. It's important to try to hold the family structure together for your own peace of mind and the future of your children. Ill-conceived actions will only bring the roof down, increase the intensity of Jack's illness and just do enormous damage all around. If he goes through with this, you obviously can't remain husband and wife, but at least there's potential for remaining good friends."

Moira agreed to stay in touch and see the doctor again in a month's time.

* * * * *

"This thing has come on us all as a huge shock," said Moira over lunch with her old law school friend, Joan Forbes, who was now well-established in a law practice. The two kept in touch on a regular basis. Joan, in fact, was godmother to Jennifer Dempster.

Joan, used to seeing family breakups at first hand, replied, "I'll bet it has. What are you going to do, leave him?"

"No, not in the sense you mean, although obviously if Jack goes ahead with this there'll be an end to the marriage. I've thought long and hard about the entire question and have consulted with Dr. Myers. She's the foremost specialist on transsexualism in the city and she knows this is no bizarre, kinky craze. It's bound up with a person's basic biology. It's deep-seated and a lifetime condition which a person is born with and only death finally lays it to rest."

"Yes, so they tell me," replied Joan, half believingly. She was less concerned with spiritual and emotional issues, and medical reasons only entered the picture as evidence when fighting a case. Her *modus operandi* as a divorce and family law specialist was to get the best settlement she could for her client. She had been brought up in a school of hard knocks when neither side expected to give any quarter beyond that required by law.

Joan became less flippant. "I've run across Dr. Myers before and there's no question she does have an excellent reputation. But, y'know, from what you tell me, you might be one in a thousand if you can bring about a peaceful, sensible and fair solution in a matter like this. Even with the hest intentions in the world, one party or the other becomes greedy and overly demanding. There's always the temptation of the one-upmanship routine – You hit me and I'll hit you back even harder, and so on."

"Yes, I realise that, but I'm relying substantially on Jack's sense of fairplay and his often expressed concern for the kids and myself which I've never had cause for doubt. You see, both he and I see it as a health issue to be treated as such. On the flip side, many people see it as a matter of immorality and irresponsibility and I suppose I can understand them saying that I have my head in the sand. But for God's sakes, if someone doesn't make an effort to undertake what I believe is called a tactical retreat, then we might as well throw our hands up and admit defeat before the battle starts.

"In the end, who am I to condemn? It might have been me with some terminal illness and then I would've had to rely on Jack's loyalty and devotion. As this is a health issue he has to rely on my loyalty and devotion and I've made up my mind not to let him down when he needs me," said Moira sensing that her friend remained at least sceptical. "I know what you're thinking, Joan."

"Oh, what am I thinking, Honey?" replied Joan, a little facetiously.

"You think I've lost my marbles."

"Oh no! Not much, but maybe just a little."

"If you do, I think you're overlooking the Rakewood case. Kathy wanted Dave Rakewood's hide and what did she end up with? She has his estate it's true, but no husband and I hear a badly strained relationship with her children which may be permanently injured," said Moira.

"Yes, I guess you were right on losing your marbles, but having said that I recognise your motives as being high-minded and I applaud you on that score. All I can say is do what you feel best, but remain very wary. You and I are Scots and they say we're very canny. That doesn't mean you have to take advantage of Jack, but it does mean that you make every move with caution and wisdom. Eventually there will have to be a divorce or annulment and a property division. If you're telling me that you want that to come last rather than first, that's okay with me so long as you keep your eyes open all the way. What d'you think you might do later? Staying at home keeping a lonely vigil is not a good answer. You'll no doubt find another husband, but I think you'd be well advised to go back to some worthwhile work," Joan advised.

"Yes, that's perfectly true. Quite apart from this I'd been thinking of taking advantage of my law degree and going back to a career. The kids will be off our hands soon and Jack and I had talked about it. I'd have to go through a refresher and then find someone to article with. It would please my dad. Dad had hoped that one of our kids might go into the profession, but I think they all have other ideas, particularly Jeremy if he ever gets his brains unscrambled."

"Well, no matter. You're doing the right thing by planning ahead. In this big world today a girl has to look after herself, so I say go for it."

Somehow, Moira felt that in spite of Joan's apparently ready acceptance of her explanation there was still a good deal of scepticism hidden underneath. She thought to herself that this was only to be expected as the scenario was so uncommon. Marital breakups for whatever reason were so frequently destructive, sometimes to the point of insanity. Well, they could think what they like, but so far as Moira was concerned this was going to be an occasion when mutual respect and common sense would still prevail. She knew that was what Jack also wanted, so, so long as there was a common accord between the two of them, this is how things could work out.

* * * * *

Moira thought about Jeremy on the way home. She still could not understand how or why he had got himself into drugs. He was really no different than the two younger kids and had in no way been singled out for special treatment or a lack of parental consideration. She knew that while he was a perfectionist he partied quite a lot after graduating from high school and while awaiting entry to university. She thought he must have got in with a fast crowd and one minor experiment with a drug might have been the start of it all. Jack had suggested that there might be a deeper psychological reason, but at the moment no one had any clue as to what it might be. Was it possible she thought that Jeremy's case was again a matter of hidden transsexuality and the challenges of dealing with a subject which reared up in front of him, as insurmountable as a great tall cliff. She had heard before that transsexuals often took refuge in alcohol or drugs and, in cases like David Rakewood he had tried to drown it out by resorting to heavy drinking which his wife, could no more tolerate than the belief that he knew he should have been a woman.

Of course in Jack's case he had not taken to drink or drugs, but he had a hiatus hernia and would probably have succumbed to stomach ulcers at the rate he was suppressing his internalized worries. She knew that theory indicated that a high proportion of teenage suicides were due to the inability of the victim to deal with their sexual orientation issues and in others it was a matter of not being able to cope with gender identity disorder. Maybe Jeremy was gay and did not know how to deal with it, even more frightening maybe he was transsexual and with two in one family that would be pretty terrifying. Added to that his ideas of what he anticipated the family would think of him could have also been a very real factor is running away from life and turning for solace to drugs. It was all a very worrying prospect for Moira and thank God for Jack in the special way that he had taken to dealing with and trying to help Jeremy.

Then there was Captain Stephen Jones. An interesting man, handsome in a rugged sort of way, blunt and to the point and not given to mincing his words. When Steve came out with an explanation it was direct and not beyond hurting one's ears and perhaps finer feelings because he dealt with things head on just like she was sure he did when he was in command of ships. But he seemed to be the right medicine for Jeremy. He had visited Jeremy in prison and while she thought that Jeremy had not got round to liking Steve she knew he respected him, never failing to address him as, "Sir."

Jack had relayed the drift of his conversations with Jeremy and Steve's activities in his behalf. Steve had talked at some length to Jeremy about working on the tugs for a while. He could sort himself out and learn to lead a healthy life with good food, interesting and challenging work which would not be easy for a novice, but with a crew who would not judge him because of his recent past mistakes. These men had in some instances been through the same experience themselves and the tug he had in mind had a particularly fine skipper who had himself lost a daughter to the drug scene. In her case she paid the ultimate price and a pretty girl had become an ugly whore before she died of disease.

Jeremy liked the idea and discussed it with his father when Jack visited him.

"What do you think Dad, Do you think I'd make a sailor?"

"If you want to, I'm sure you can. You might even find it so much to your liking that you make a lifetime career out of it. Many have done that before you and they say once the sea is in your blood you never lose it." replied Jack.

"I think I've shaken the drug habit and I've had some counselling while I've been inside. I know there will always be the temptation to fall off the wagon, as they say about alcoholics."

"Never mind that, You'll do okay so long as you keep your eyes on your objectives. Your mother and I are right behind you and never forget that. Steve will be there to help and advise you and his friend Captain Collins has agreed to have you on his boat. He's a good skipper from whom you'll learn a lot. You'll go as an unpaid extra hand by arrangement with the tug owners to see if you like it and if the skipper finds you have potential, they'll probably hire you and then you can start earning regular wages. When you're off duty your room will always be available at home. It'll give you time to think. Maybe you will want to sign on for architecture at university or maybe you'll find the tugs so attractive that you'll become a captain yourself one day."

"Oh, by the way." said Jeremy, "I had another visitor two days ago. Her name is Elaine, a social worker in training. Her full name is Elaine Rakewood of the well-known family of that name. She was a hippie but has given that up. Seems to be quite a nice girl, who says she would like to help me when I get out. She's working towards a master's degree. Interesting huh?"

"Yes, very interesting indeed. I'll watch her progress with interest. Elizabeth Sadler is her father's sister, so we had heard that she was considering a career." replied Jack.

* * * * *

At this point, the Reverend George Marley re-entered Jack's life. The phone rang. It was Rev. Marley calling from the

United Church. There was the usual exchange of greetings for the minister and Jack Dempster had become quite cordial after their initial meeting some months earlier. "Jack, it's good to be talking with you again. Do you have a moment or two."

"Yes, George I certainly do. What can I do for you?" replied Jack.

"We're having an informal get-together of maybe half a dozen clerics from the four mainline churches in this neighbourhooed. The purpose is to discuss the problems of youth and the drug culture today, because as you know a number of people in this affluent area have lost kids to the street life and drugs. The churches have taken a back seat on this issue and we want to explore what can or should be done about it from the churches point of view. We also have a non-conformist minister, a gentleman by the name of Clive Jenkins coming along. Mr. Jenkins has done a lot of work in the Downtown Eastside and knows your son, Jeremy."

"Sounds like an interesting idea, but things have moved ahead in my private life quite considerably since we last saw you for a heart-to-heart talk. I think we should get together again for a one-on-one a little ahead of meeting your colleagues," replied Jack.

The following night they met in Reverend Marley's study alongside the church. Jack sat down comfortably and without the feeling of foreboding he had when they had their last chat.

"Well, George, since we last talked quite a lot has happened. First, Moira, my wife is fully in the picture on my gender identity problem. It came as a huge shock to her as I expected, but I think we are going to be able to work through it without too much damage. It's going to take time and patience, but she sees the need for a unified approach on it as we deal with the rest of the family."

"I'm certainly pleased to hear that. It must be like getting rid of a heavy load off your mind. And what about your son?"

"Jeremy you mean. He's doing ninety days in prison so that has given us a bit of a respite from the constant nagging worry about his condition on the street. He was nabbed as an accessory to an assault. Whether he had any real intent is doubtful as he was badly under the influence at the time, but they seem to work to protect each other's backs and when a friend of mine approached Jeremy the other one moved into the attack. The other guy was arrested on an assault charge and Jeremy got picked up with him. In many ways it was a blessing in disguise as it has at least broken the cycle of dependency while he's been inside. The true test will arise when he's released so that's what we are working on now, in an effort to keep him away from the drug culture permanently."

Rev. Marley then turned to his proposed informal meeting. "What we are proposing to do is to have an initial meeting with my opposite numbers from the Anglican, Lutheran, R.C. and maybe a couple of others. I'll be representing the United Church. We want to discuss the central problem of drug addiction, how it affects families, what family influences might have had on the child and what if anything can be done about it. We hope that you might be able to speak to the position of yourself as a parent and we hope Mr. Jenkins will address the subject from the standpoint of a frontline social worker. We know he has a theological degree and a degree in psychology, although he has no church affiliation. I think most of the clerics believe that their churches must contribute more than just hand-wringing."

"That means he has no official line to uphold, I'd presume. I'd say that's an advantage given the type of work he does. The people he ministers to all have a rebellious point-of-view. They're against the establishment and its institutions, against authority, against any show of wealth which they see as only something to be plundered and so on," mused Jack.

"I think you've got it about right," replied the minister.

"How far is this likely to go, George? Will it be a sort of flash in the pan or do you see it as being a movement that will gather force and effectiveness as it goes."

"It's hard to tell. It will depend on what effort people are prepared to put out. If it's just the comfortable pew routine, or not in my backyard attitude, then it won't go anywhere. People in some instances are genuinely afraid. They're concerned for their younger children. They don't want a thief to be part of their household. The addicted offspring is so desperate for his or her next fix, they'll do anything to get it. The boys steal and the girls turn to prostitution and for most, once they reach a certain critical point, there's no road back. It may be idealism on my part, but I'm prepared to roll up my sleaves and get my hands dirty to help those who are capable of being saved for a better life. Others, I have to recognise have gone too far and are beyond any sort of redemption," said the minister his voice reflecting his sombre mood.

"George, that sums up our experience with Jeremy. If we loose him when he comes out he'll be right back to his street life in a matter of minutes. He's to be discharged to our custody and if Moira and I can't field it properly with help from others, then we'll have to kiss him goodbye forever.... He won't come back and we won't be able to tolerate having him back. That's what we've had to brace ourselves for." Jack replied.

"Your story, miserable and heart-breaking though it is, is typical and that's why I thought it would be a real help that my colleagues meet an actual parent with the experiencc. If we can develop a step by-step strategy my hope is that we can expand it into a bigger and wider public meeting or series of public meetings until we can hammer a project or some projects together to do something practical that will help these kids. We know that old fashioned preaching will go nowhere. We have to do something practical to capture their hearts and imaginations and then by that route we might be able to deal with their souls. This is not going to be a heavy religious reawakening project. The kids, if they have any savvy will quickly figure that one out for themselves once the drug clouds have cleared away."

"Does anyone know about my gender identity problem and what I'm doing about it, George?" Jack asked.

"Absolutely not. You approached me with it as a matter of confidentiality and I treated it that way. How you wish to treat it now it is coming out into the open with your family, is entirely up to you. However, if you want to cover it in any way when the little group I've formed is together would be okay with me. it would, I suggest, make an interesting topic for discussion. I have talked informally with my colleagues about transsexuality in a general way, but have indicated nothing to do with any specific person. Reactions as you'll guess were pretty mixed, privately sympathetic in most instances, but officially reflecting the dogma of their churches. A lot is bound up in this same-sex marriage business, and some, despite the legal and medical treatment, continue to view it as a cosmetic procedure without any change of sex or gender in reality."

"I don't mind talking about it to an intelligent receptive audience. It's something I'll have to face in my professional life, whether its the partnership or the staff at my engineering consultancy, or whether it's professional groups or the public at large, because there are occasions when we have to explain a major project at public hearings. This may be an opportunity to get my feet wet, as they say," replied Jack hopefully.

* * * * *

The first of several meetings took place at the United Church office. All who attended had been asked to keep it informal and low key. Jack knew none of the participants except for Reverend George Marley and after introductions had been made, everyone settled down in their chairs expectantly. The only exception to the informal garb that they all wore was Father Patrick O'Sully, a bluff Irishman who was also probably the oldest there.

He said "I'm not going to apologise for being the only one here who is actually wearing clerical clothes, but that is on account of the fact that I wear nothing else regardless of the weather and don't actually possess a collar and tie. The Catholic church as you know tends to be very conservative about its dress code and at my age, I'm unlikely to change."

"So be it, Father Patrick. Let's all join hands and ask the Lord's blessing as an opener," said Reverend Marley.

"Lord God Almighty, we ask thy blessings on this meeting of thine servents and prey that out of our deliberations, much good will flow to the benefit of our congregations and their children. We believe Lord, that youth is in a state of crisis and we pray you will show us the correct path by which we will be able to help improve their situation and cure them of the evils of alcohol and harmful drugs. At the end of this meeting we pray that we will all go our separate ways, united with a common purpose to help these children and their families. Amen"

The discussion covered a wide area as each of them spoke of problems they had come up against that related to the central subject of drug addiction among youth. Jack sat next to Clive Jenkins and found in him a man he could relate to. Clive was a tall, tanned and rangy sort of guy who wore cowboy boots and a leather tie around his neck which somehow typed him as a man from the country. He reminded Jack of the late actor Gary Cooper as he spoke with a deep voice which was surprisingly gentle. He described the work he did among youth in the Downtown Eastside and how it was an uphill battle for all concerned.

"Poverty is an industry in the Downtown Eastside" remarked Clive. "There are a great many agencies all working in the supposed common good but generally the effort is spread very thin as they all compete for the same government largesse, which has never been overly generous and now is particularly restricted as governement tries to correct some of the excesses of the past. When I refer to poverty as being an industry, I'm not talking about the poor specifically, I'm talking of those who invent a scheme supposedly meant to help some disadvantaged group or another. They develop a budget which includes generous salaries for the promoters. Somehow this salary is bracketted with other supposed expenses so that while the apparent salary might be quite small, the real draw down of expenses and other advantages in the way of travel, car and a variety of supposed needs flows into the private pockets of the promoters."

"Can you be more specific, Mr. Jenkins and give us some examples?" asked Reverend Hubert Schimmel from the Lutheran church.

"Oh, yes, there are a number which have either folded or simply closed their doors when funding was cut off. This, of course, is always accompanied by much screaming of unfairness to the particular group, but from my experience they sooner or later bring it upon themselves. One such was an organization that was closed two or three years ago. It had been set up to provide a shelter and canteen for what they called street-engaged transgendered people who commonly functioned as prostitutes in an effort to feed their drug habit while they also tried to live out their lives in their adopted sex. By informed experts there might have been a maximum of fifty functioning full time on the street with perhaps another fifty who came in and out of the street scene, but did not necessarily need the sort of help the society was offering," Clive advised.

"What was the scale of help they gave?" asked Reverend Herbert Fawcett from the Anglican church.

"Basically, a shower and laundry facility, a limited menu mostly made up of soups, hamburgers and fries and some fresh fruit. They could also use a small lounge and watch television. There was a limited used clothing supply but no lodging. It was open from ten in the morning with fresh coffee and closed by six in the evening. They started with a taxpayer funding of about $200,000 which climbed to $300,000 so divide that between about

30 or 40 people served on average and it comes out to about six or seven thousand per year per head," Clive replied.

"That's a lot of money and you say much of it flowed into the hands of the promoters." remarked Father O'Sully.

"Yes, that's about it. Eventually it collapsed but it was hushed up. If it had ever made the newspapers it would have been another small, but highly potent scandal, which hurts the genuine charities."

Clive described the nature of the work that he undertook in helping young drug addicts. "I work with a man named Stephen Jones. Steve provides the tough love element and I work in the kindness and succour department. We are assisted by a few volunteers, but frankly, we usually can only seriously help the new arrivals before the damage becomes too extensive. Once they have passed a certain point, living on the street, malnutrition has set in and they don't want any help. They only want their fixes. It's only possible to turn them around if they will let you and if you can get them away from their environment long enough to effect a reasonable rehabilitation."

At this point Jack Dempster broke in. "Clive and Steve are known to me, particularly Steve. They helped with my son Jeremy who is presently in prison and is due for release shortly." There was momentary shock on the faces of some present as Jack continued. "We have a job for him to go to which will take him to sea, which is about the only safe place we can think of where he'll be away from the bad elements long enough to hopefully shake the habit."

The night was wearing on and it was obvious that there was a great deal more to discuss, but the response from the attending clergymen was one of great interest and all agreed that they should continue the discussion in a week or so when everyone found it convenient.

In the meantime Jack and Clive agreed to have lunch after the latter had said, "Jack I understand you're an engineer. I'd very much like to talk with you about a project that is very close to my heart."

* * * * *

Chapter Nine

The Choice is Unity

Several days later Moira sat at her kitchen table, enjoying a cigarette over a mid-morning cup of coffee. She was not a calculating woman in the sense that she sought to take advantage of others, but she was inherently canny and non-committal in the manner of her Scottish ancestors. She thought out the many aspects of the future of the marriage, her husband's and her own future and the future of their children in the light of the revelations made about Jack's dilemma. There was also the matter of interfamily relationships to consider, her widower father and Jack's parents, and the shock effect the news would have on them.

That she loved Jack was not in question, even now. From her point of view their marriage had been a happy one. Jack was a dutiful husband, a good and considerate lover and a caring father to the children, As a qualified professional he was a partner in a well-known, established firm of consulting engineers and his future seemed assured. On the one hand, she reasoned, why would a man give up all these hallmarks of personal success and fulfillment for an uncertain future as a sex changed woman? He would suffer stigma, be ostracized, criticized, cruelly lampooned and have rejection to contend with. All of this could come from everyone he knew, his children, his and her family, their friends and neighbours, his business associates and clients and, of course, most importantly, Moira herself.

It struck her as being an enormous price to pay for simply being born in the wrong sex. She reasoned that for most of us the idea of being anything other than the way we were born would be totally foreign. She accepted her own female role without any question or doubt whatsoever. She liked men, but she could never imagine herself as being one of them. There were pains involved in being a woman and when things went badly there could be emotional traumas such as few men even knew existed.

On the other hand there were countless little pleasures and some big ones as well. She thought of the moments of joy when her children were first placed in her arms; the bonding of mother to child seemed immediate and encompassed everything she thought of at that time. She remembered the sensation as she breast-fed them and recalled how she marvelled at the tiny features and how she then pictured them as grown up people of the future. There were pains and setbacks, Jeremy's recent troubles with drugs being the worst but otherwise they were healthy bright kids and for that she was thankful.

She took stock of her own feelings in the matter. No, she did not like Jack's news and, yes, it had been as much of a shock and came with as little warning as an earthquake. She could see how devastating and acrimonious, probably even scandalous, a marital breakup could be if mismanaged. It would mean changed relationships and possibly selling the lovely home for which they had worked very hard together. Hostility within the family could be destructive if allowed to take hold and he might lose his source of income if his partners turned against him.

In several sessions she had with Dr. Margaret Myers and her partner Dr. George Fellowes she had come to realize just how central she was to the entire matter. She could, like Samson, pull down the pillars of the temple and quickly destroy the marriage, or she could render support to her husband so that their relationship could be re-channelled and take new form so that both could still function within limits as parents and later as grandparents. If they presented a united front in breaking all this to their children and relatives, removal of at least some bones of contention might make the matter all that easier to handle.

She wondered about Jack's friendship with this new friend of his, Linda Bowker. If their marriage was indeed going to be dissolved, she supposed it could not matter too much. If a dissolution of the marriage happened, she knew she was still very much of marriageable age and felt herself to be still attractive. How would Jack feel if he knew that she was marriage bound? She supposed there might be some pang of jealousy as she was currently feeling in regard to Linda. She knew she had no one in view and it was very premature to even consider such a possibility. On the other hand, she had an obligation to take into account her own interests, no matter what sacrifice she may have to make in helping Jack.

When she mentioned in passing that Dr. Myers had told her a little of Linda Bowker, she was watchful for Jack's reaction. He merely smiled and said "Oh, yes, she helped me with my first lesson in fully cross-dressing and make-up. I see her periodically for a coffee or a bite of lunch, but have no fear, my dear, there's nothing other than a very ordinary friendship involved with someone who can help me over some of the rough spots in handling this. After all, she's been through it herself so her experience is helpful and helps my understanding."

Moira felt reassured. There was no trace of embarrassment or hiding of guilt. Jack had never ever tried to deceive her, and even with his recent revelations she had come to realize the true nature of his problem and no longer regarded that as deception.

She recalled suggesting that she would like to meet Linda. "I'll ask her if she'd like to come round then," replied Jack. In the next few days this was to happen.

* * * * *

Moira's mother had passed away some years before and her father, a retired law professor, lived alone in a nice condominium surrounded by his books. He had been a specialist in aviation and maritime law and was now writing a book on the subject. As her thinking crystallized, the thought of going into the legal profession became more and more attractive to Moira. This way she could assure her independence and during a session with her father she explored the idea a little further. He was the first person with whom she discussed the problem, outside of the doctors and her friend Joan Forbes and he pointed out a few legal aspects.

"Moira, I'm no happier than you are about all this, but I'm sufficiently knowledgeable about it all to know that one can't blame Jack for a condition he was likely born with. He's in a real box or dilemma. Probably what he's doing about it all is best for him. Be thankful that he hasn't taken refuge in the bottle or drugs or some other bad habit to drown out his sorrows.

"He has to change everything," Moira's father continued. "You have to adjust your attitude and make plans for your own security, in much the same way as if you'd learned that he was terminally ill. I know there's a feeling of bereavement here. It is inevitable and something which the children also have to face up to and then there's the added complication of Jeremy. But compare it to the shock you would have had if he'd had a fatal fall at a project or been in an horrendous car or plane crash.

"I appreciate very fully that there is the breaking of what appeared to be a very secure marital bond and that it adds up to a terrible wrench. Truly, its the death of the marriage, and effectively a husband, a life-long partner, a lover and so forth, has been knocked in the head. On the other hand, at least with this problem, the two of you can work your way together through all this using the wisdom of both of you. For example, if the children know that you are supportive, Moira my dear, and there's no schism between the two of you, they won't feel that their security has been totally undermined.

"Also, if you're with him when he tells his firm and proclaim your solidarity with him, they'll at least know that they are not dealing with a disastrous marital breakup at the same time."

Moira's father paused and then carried on with his wise dissertation. "Now, let's suppose that Jack goes through to a full sex change and re-registers his birth. This can be done in Canada retroactively to birth date, so that the apparent evidence is that he was always female. But in this country two people of the same sex cannot remain married to each other.* You could do one of three things: (a) take no action, in which case your marriage would effectively be *ultra vires,* or without further force or effect, (b) you could divorce on grounds that your conjugal rights have been lost; or (c) you could formally apply for an annulment. Any way you do it there's an inevitable change in your relationship. To do nothing is not really the best way as it could be termed an unofficial annulment, the end result being precisely the same except that it might leave a fair number of legal loose ends to tie up. I would advise a formal annulment, as you could clean up these other aspects at the same time.

"Jack may also remain living with you on a 'best friends' basis if you are both in agreement. He is still the children's father and nothing can alter that. As such he will remain responsible for providing for them and yourself, even if separated, as long as you remain dependent. Of course he can also expect to have visitation rights if you don't stay together."

"There'll be other loose ends to tie up. What to do with registered retirement plans is one? Another will have to do with the changed circumstances in ownership of the house, not that either name comes off the title, but there will be a change in the relative position of both of you in going from 'joint tenants' to

* As at the last date of correction the issue of same sex marriage in Canada is being settled. The Supreme Court has been asked to rule on this issue although same sex marriages are already being performed in some provinces.

'tenants in common.' Then again there will be the matter of beneficial interests in life insurance policies. All these things can be dealt with under capable legal advice. But for God' sakes, both of you, keep away from the divorce mills. Those people make their living out of turning marital breakups into bar room brawls," said her father.

Moira was grateful for her father's input. "Dad, how do you think you'll react to Jack becoming a woman?"

"It's hard to tell. At the moment I feel very sorry for you all, perhaps in the sense that Jack, as we know him, is dying. But the new Jackie might well be a very attractive person well worth knowing. It's a mistake to assume that deterioration is inevitable. I did read somewhere that a better person can also result, not that I ever found Jack to be a bad son-in-law. Have you seen him dressed up?"

"Yes, twice in the privacy of our bedroom. He looks surprisingly good, really quite attractive in a feminine sense, and yet I can't see him changing much in other regards," said Moira.

"No, of course not. He's still going to have the same intellectual skills, the same brain, the same skeleton, although he obviously has to change in terms of his body and emotions and the superficial things to do with appearance. No doubt his responses and attitudes will become more feminine, which is the way it has to be if he's to succeed as a woman. What about you, Moira? What will you do?"

"My inclination is to stay with Jack through all this. I'll go back to law school for a refresher course and then hope to article. My good friend Joan Forbes, has said she will article me."

"Oh, yes, I remember Joan quite well. She was a very good student."

"I know she has a successful practice in family law which would interest me greatly." Moira volunteered. "I've discussed the idea with Jack and he's very much in favour. It remains for us to break the news to the children, but Jeremy's situation might complicate things. He's due out of prison in a few days. I've been to visit him with Jack and he seems to have learned a great deal about cleaning up his act and his life; the acid test will come when he's released into our custody. Then there's Jack's mother and father. I think she'll understand, but Jack's father being very much of the old school, ex-air force, ex-RCMP and all that, might be a more difficult one to deal with."

"Well, I wish you both lots of luck. When Jack wants to discuss it with me, tell him I'm not going to be hard to deal with, and I'll lend him a sympathetic ear."

"Thanks, Dad for being such a wise and wonderful father," said Moira, leaning over to give him a kiss as she got ready to leave. She was now in tears, but quickly composed herself as Lyle gave her a firm hug.

* * * * *

Jennifer at 19 and Joshua two years her junior were intelligent, fairly serious-minded children who got on well with each other and their parents. Jack had patiently explained to his children all the facets and factors in his condition and why he was having to deal with it at long last after years of secrecy and repression.

Joshua had suggested that, as his father had kept it secret for so long, why didn't he just go on doing that.

"That's what I would have done if I hadn't become so tormented and anguished. Sleeping a nightmare when unconscious is bad enough, but when you can't even be honest with yourself, it's a living hell from which there's no escape until you confront the whole mess head-on and deal with it. After you've been honest with yourself, the next thing is to be honest with other people and that's why we're talking today. I have to be honest with you as the next step in dealing with my problem. I can't bottle it all up for ever in silent secrecy. I have to relate to other people and try to normalize my life."

"Does that mean that you'll be leaving and you two will be splitting up?" asked Jennifer.

At this point Moira intervened. "No, darling, it doesn't. Dad is staying here while he goes through his change and I'm in full support of what he has to do for the sake of his mental health." Moira took her husband's hand. "Of course there are a lot of things that have to be worked out, but Dad and I are reasonable people and we still love each other and always will.

"What about Jeremy? How are you going to deal with him," asked Jennifer. Both kids were concerned about their brother but knew that he was going to need some special handling.

"Jeremy will be coming out of prison in a few days and we're going to bring him home before he goes away on a tugboat that Captain Jones has arranged. We have to get him kitted out with sea boots and work clothes because this is no joy ride he is going on. Mum and I have seen him while he has been inside and so has Captain Jones and we both agree that there has been a huge improvement in his attitude. But it's not going to be easy for him, temptation will be there and if the drug dealers can get their hands on him when he comes out they'll see that more dope is available to him so that they can get him hooked again. It will only take one shot to do it." said Jack.

"Are you going to tell him about your sex change," asked Joshua.

"We will, but it will be a little early yet," said Moira. "We need to see that he has recovered from his addiction to a better extent first. We don't know how he'll react. It could set him back, but also it could be good for him in another sense because it'll show how another person in the family, your Dad, has handled his problem without turning to drugs or alcohol."

"I take it we should not give him any clue that such a thing is happening, but we will be free to discuss it with him after you have told him, right" asked Jennifer.

"Yes, that's right," answered Moira. "We think it's important to hold the home together and provide you two with a secure base to work from. Isn't it better this way than one of you stumbling onto the situation by accident and having no one to help you understand? You are all a product of our love for each other, as is this home and even though there are lots of challenges ahead for all of us, I believe we can get through it all okay as a family."

Jennifer started to cry. She walked over to her father sobbing, "Daddy, I still love you no matter what. You're my father, that can never change, and I do want you to know that I'll support you and Mom through this ordeal. I think Mom is being very wise by showing understanding and support. If she had been the opposite this home and this family could have been in ruins by now."

Her father lifted her face, gave her a gentle kiss and then drew her tightly to his chest. In the meantime, Joshua had moved over to his mother, took her hands between his. His eyes were moist and his chin trembled as he fought back years. He said, "Don't worry, Mom, Jennifer and I are going to stand by you both and to heck with what the rest of the world thinks."

* * * * *

Clive Jenkins and Jack had lunch together the week after the meeting with the clergymen.

"How did you react to the meeting Jack? I gather you had only known George Marley before it. Right?"

"Yes, that's right. I thought the meeting was quite progressive and shows that some of the churches realize that there is a massive social problem which is not confined to Vancouver alone.

It's so widespread, it's like a cancer that's eating away at civilization as we know it. How about you?"

"That's about the way I see it also. Society generally has to realize that we're all involved in this thing and its cure, if that's still possible. We can't expect government to do it for us. With a population of 30 million I wonder just how many people live off the drug based crime and how many it serves. If we had any figures I'll guarantee it would scare the pants off millions of us," said Clive.

"What I wanted to mention to you is the fact that I own an old homestead up in the Cariboo. It's where I was brought up and where my parents lived out their lives. As the only surviving offspring it was left to me by my Dad. He had not lived there for some years and now I have a tenant in the place. I've long harboured the idea that the property might be an ideal place to establish a camp along the lines of the Twin Valleys project in Ontario."

"Oh, what was Twin Valleys?" asked Jack. "I've never heard of it."

"It was a project that was started up by a man named George Bullied around 1970. It was a great success in rehabilitating strung out, disaffected druggies from the youth population. I think the same thing could be done with my property, but it needs someone with engineering skills to lay it out. There's no power to it at the moment but there is an excellent water source that could be used for power generation and also water storage for irrigation in the summer, as it can be very dry there for a couple on months. But I need professional help and I hoped that I could gain your interest."

"We'd have to take a look at it, and I would be prepared to do that over some weekend in the near future if that's what you have in mind, Clive," replied Jack. "However, there's one thing I meant to mention at the meeting we had the other day with the clergymen, but we'd ran out of time."

"Oh, what was that?" asked Clive just mildly curious.

"You mentioned that society that was set up for transgendered, street-engaged people."

"Yes, I remember that."

"Well, you should know that I'm transgendered, or more particularly, transsexual and I'm in the process of change," said Jack, his voice radiating confidence.

Clive's expression was a study. It was as though his facial muscles had frozen, just at the time when he was going to place another fork full of food in his mouth. "Did I hear you correctly, my friend?"

"Yes, you did. I'm a transsexual in process of change. I thought it was best you know, now before we get into any serious discussions on your camp idea, which incidentally I like, but I can't work with you under false pretences. If you don't like what I have told you and want to drop the subject of your camp, now's the time to do so," came the reply.

"I'll admit you took me totally by surprise, but I'm flattered that you told me so directly. After all we are almost strangers and it will need time to sink in. But on the other hand I admire your courage and suspect you'll handle it very well," said Clive.

"I don't mind admitting that the biggest hurdle is past me. I had to tell my wife and it was something I had been fearing for months. It came as a terrible shock to her, but happily she's thought it out and is standing by me. That's the only reason I've suddenly found my confidence so you're about the first outside of family that I've told."

* * * * *

The weeks rolled by at a surprising speed. Jeremy came out of prison and had worked well and diligently on the tugboats. His vessel took him on a variety of trips as far away as the Queen Charlotte Islands and to the West Coast of Vancouver Island. With plenty of hard work, good food and watch duties his appetite had recovered. Captain Collins gave him a good report after his first two trips and from then on he was taken on the payroll as a deck-hand. He was now starting to feel he had a future and could see that tugboat work offered him good prospects for getting ahead. Captain Collins with an understanding of Jeremy's background problem treated him like a son, always explaining things and giving him good advice. When they came into Vancouver, Collins always took pains to be sure that Jeremy would go straight home and would not be tempted to visit Main and Hastings.

In fact the tugboat office would call the Dempster home to let the family know that someone could be at the company dock to pick up Jeremy and drive him home. Usually it was Moira who did this, but on occasion Jennifer would deal with it. The practice in the tugboat business was that the tug would be out for about two weeks each trip and then an alternative crew would take over for the next trip which meant that Jeremy had time off. Jack encouraged him to get back to his books and study something useful and worthwhile when at home. After several trips Jeremy announced that when he had the necessary qualifying sea time in, he intended to go to Nautical School in North Vancouver with the aim of getting his coastal mate's ticket.

Jeremy still had no idea about his father's change until Jack and Moira took him aside and explained what was going on. The shock was profound and for a moment Jack was alarmed at his reaction. Jeremy burst into tears and after gathering his composure came out with a remark that surprised them both

"Thank God, there's someone in this family who is not perfect. I thought I was the only one who carried guilty secrets. In fact it made me so miserable thinking I had to compete with perfection and recognizing that I couldn't keep up. I think when I tried dope it took away the feeling of inferiority and after that it didn't take long to become hooked."

"Was that what it was all about?" asked Moira suddenly relieved of a great burden.

"Yes, I think so," replied Jeremy. "I don't feel inferior any more. I know I'm doing a good job of work and the skipper and the rest of the crew seem to like me. And now when I'm home I appreciate it, instead of having that terrible feeling that I must get away from it at all costs.

"How do you feel about your Dad's sex change, then, Jeremy," asked Moira with some apprehension.

Jeremy chose his words with care. "I couldn't have been more surprised, but on the other hand if that's what turns you on, Dad, its okay with me."

"It's not a matter of being turned, son. It's a matter of survival, difficult though it might be to understand," said Jack.

"Well, that's what I wanted to say It's the kinda subject that gets me all tongue-tied. What I meant is that it's okay by me. I understand it's a health issue. You helped me through the drug thing and I'll do whatever I can to help you," replied Jeremy.

Jeremy drew a deep breath and held it as if he was getting ready to let something out. Now it was the Dempster's turn to be surprised. "I have something to tell you."

"Oh, do let us know" said Moira.

"I'm seeing Elaine Rakewood and you might say we are going steady. She visited me in prison as I told you Dad, and now the chemistry between us is good and strong. She was into soft drugs when she was in hippieland, but has changed her whole attitude to them, partly because she is intent on doing social work and something useful for society and, partly because she saw the bloody mess they made of my life. She has helped me a lot and now I have something and someone to look forward to outside the home. In fact we are going out for dinner tomorrow night and hopefully on a lot of other occasions."

"Are you in love then, son?" asked Jack.

"Yes, I believe I am. I know we look forward to seeing each other, each time I come home."

"Good, congratulations and I hope it all works out for the two of you. Have you met her mother yet?" said Moira.

"No, I have not been invited to her mother's home yet. I know there have been lots of problems between Elaine and Mrs. Rakewood, but Elaine has her own apartment. It seems better that way," replied Jeremy.

Later when Jeremy had gone out to meet Elaine, Moira remarked to Jack.

"I guess we gave Jeremy a big surprise tonight, but his news for us was nearly as big a surprise to me. Of all people imagine us being related by marriage to a Rakewood, although I suspect Elaine is more like her father than her mother."

"Yes, it was a big surprise, but it could be the best news yet. A happy marriage may be the best antidote there could be for our son."

* * * * *

Moira was doing a refresher course at law school and finding it interesting and enjoyable, but hard work nonetheless. Jackie was now dressing quite openly at home and would sometimes go out in the evening. Moira had even been out shopping with her, although they judged it better that they travel to shopping centres unlikely to be frequented by their friends and contemporaries. Linda had not yet visited, but today she was due to come around for dinner.

There was a ring at the door which Jackie answered, letting her friend in. Moira came out of the kitchen to meet Linda. "Hi, Linda, it's so nice to meet you." They shook hands. "Naturally, I've heard quite a lot about you." Linda reciprocated with her own greeting, "Moira, it's very nice to meet you, also," she said as the two shook hands.

Moira was immediately impressed with Linda's tall slender figure. She towered above Moira by several inches. Her attractiveness was undeniable. It was hard to imagine that she had once been a man. It was certainly encouraging that such a transformation was possible, at least, she supposed, when seen through Jackie's eyes.

Linda felt a little uncomfortable, as if she was being appraised, for what she could only imagine. Perhaps Moira had invited her over to see what sort of adversary she might be facing for Jack's affections. The thought was ludicrous, she thought to herself. She knew which way he was travelling and accepted that. She felt no attraction towards women beyond simple friendship. She was not opposed to them, she was with them all the way and like any heterosexual woman directed her gaze in the direction of heterosexual men.

As Linda looked at Jackie, attractively dressed in a casual beige outfit, she could see little of the former man. Jackie was wearing a wig, as she still had to revert to Jack for attendance at the office, but the date of that switch was coming closer by the day and then Jack would be lost from view forever.

Jackie, for her part, looked at both women companions with very mixed thoughts. On several occasions she had discussed the wisdom of inviting Linda over. By prearrangement, she left Moira and Linda together for half an hour while she dealt with something in her den-bedroom.

After Jackie had excused herself, Moira said, "You must be speculating in your mind, Linda, as to why I invited you over for dinner. There are several reasons, quite apart from wanting to meet you. I find you to be a very attractive woman. Jackie has told me of your interesting history and I must say I admire you for the way you set about rebuilding your life and making something worthwhile out of it. I think Jackie has learned much that is good from you and has found you to be an inspiration."

"It's nice of you to say that," replied Linda.

"I suppose, in a way, the main reason is that I want to invite you quite freely into our family circle. This might sound quite strange to you, as most marriages are in ruins by this stage of a transsexual change. However, in fairness I think I can claim that Jackie and I have handled things differently to the norm. Jackie is an intensely loyal person, who has gone through her own particular meat grinder.

"The suicide of David Rakewood had a most profound effect on her and at one time might have even provoked her into suicide. I also have had many challenges over this: children, family, home, a career for myself and so on. In the end Jackie and I, knowing the marriage could not survive, decided to dismantle it in an orderly, civilized fashion, rather than bring in a bulldozer and simply wreck it, ourselves and the many relationships which are affected. I'll always love the memory of Jack. He and I are parents of three fine children. But I decided that love was better than hatred in my dealings with the emerging Jackie. I can't say I love Jackie in any romantic sense, but I'm very fond of her and see her as a close friend for the rest of our lives. I know you've also come to be a good friend of hers. So rather than fencing in the dark and wondering and imagining probably quite silly and inaccurate thoughts, I thought I'd like to get to know you as a friend."

"My gosh, Moira, you're a cool one," replied Linda. "I mean that as a compliment," she added hastily. "I don't think I have ever met anyone quite as sensible and open as you are. In fact, I doubt if many exist anywhere. You're right, there's so much anger and emotion bound up in this condition and people seem to go out of their way to do maximum damage to each other. But, y'know, when reason and common sense take over, many of life's problems shrink down to size very quickly. Jackie is a friend whom I value. Nothing more and nothing less and, I believe that goes for her also. Yes, I would be delighted to be regarded as a family friend and get to know you all. From what Jackie tells me, you've all stood by her through this. She gives the main credit to you Moira, whom she describes as about the wisest person alive. I know she's gone through hell over this and readily acknowledges that if you'd taken the same attitude as that unfortunate Rakewood woman, it would have destroyed her like it did David Rakewood. What a tragedy! What a waste!"

"Yes, that was a tragedy, "Moira responded. "Mrs. Rakewood will have it in her memory forever and I hear it has caused her many problems particularly with her children. I think that's what brought it home to me that there had to be a better way of handling this type of thing."

Jackie returned to the living room and rejoined the conversation.

"I heard the Rakewood name as I came in. I think that event will haunt me for the rest of my life," said Jackie.

"Put it behind you, love," said Moira kindly. "The world is littered with personal tragedies and life still has to go on."

"Yes, I have," said Jackie. "It's stupid to let it get you down. But, I don't think I shall ever forget the feeling of overwhelming sickness I briefly felt when I read all the details. I read of another man's problems, made the worse because I knew him and staring back, in phantom newsprint, was my own name! It shook me up very badly."

"You don't have to worry about that now or ever again," said Linda. "Moira and myself have had a good talk and she's made me welcome in your family circle. That's a most generous gesture and shows the full measure of Moira's humanity and compassion. I admire her greatly."

"That's wonderful and about what I expected," said Jackie as Moira prepared to serve dinner. "She's a wonderful person and has really shown the way to other people. Y'know, Linda, we're not hiding this thing any longer. All the immediate family have been told, my firm knows and awaits Jackie's arrival with expectancy and support. Only the other day Rakewood's lawyer, Simon Guthrie and his wife Peggy visited to meet the "new me." The generosity of intelligent people knows few limits when they are fully in the picture and understand. Peggy knows Kathy Rakewood very well. In fact she stayed with the Guthries for several days following the inquest. As Peggy said, Mrs. Rakewood still doesn't get it. I guess some people are chained to their hang-ups and prejudices and Kathy Rakewood is one of them."

* * * * *

Jack had to deal with others beyond the immediate family. His sister Marion, the nurse, was even more accepting than he had dared hope and gave Jackie words of encouragement.

"I deal with sick people all the time. For a great many, illness is just the progression of life through to death. But there are people who die needlessly through self-neglect and abuse. Take the heavy smoker who develops lung cancer. He chose to take to tobacco and never felt the need to brace up while still healthy and kick the habit. When he dies everybody feels sorry for him and society willingly pays for his mistake through health insurance. We forget that everyone has a duty and obligation to look after themselves and their health.

"As far as I'm concerned that's what you're doing. Ten days in a psychiatric ward with severe depression can cost as much as reassignment surgery. Society, in the form of health insurance, would rather pay for the depression case and let the devil look after the funding to pay for the reassignment case. Who's likely to recover first? Not the depression case, as depression can only be cured on a gradual basis. I say, go for it Jack. It isn't as though you're doing something rash or light-hearted. This has been with you all your life!"

It was a different situation with brother Bert and his wife, Maureen, both of whom had slipped into Vancouver from the Fraser Valley to visit his parents. Hugh and Mary Dempster had told their younger son about Jack but, not unnaturally the telling was so short that it had no chance of being understood. There was blood in Bert's eyes when he and his wife showed up unannounced on the Dempster's doorstep. Daughter Jennifer let them in, but as soon as the greetings were over the mood of things changed.

"Dad tells me that you're changing sex, Jack. What the hell is this all about?" asked a clearly irritated Bert.

Moira did not like the tone of this opening question and moved over to sit by Jack on the chesterfield. Jack stayed calm as he confirmed their father's statement.

"What the hell, have you gone gay or something? What are you going to do about Jeremy? I suppose you're abandoning him. Are you?" asked Bert very aggressively.

"No, I haven't gone gay and no one is abandoning Jeremy, least of all me. But if you relax for the next several minutes I'd like to give you a proper explanation."

"I'm not interested in goddamned explanations. I know what a transsexual is. We run into them all the time. They're a bunch of gays who've gone wacky in the head. Almost all of them choose prostitution and many are infected with HIV. I never thought a brother of mine would choose this as a way of life!"

"And I never thought a brother of mine, supposedly an intelligent man, would demonstrate so quickly just what an ignorant bugger he really is. Bert, if you haven't got the courtesy and decency to listen, there's nothing I can say that's going to get through to that bag of sawdust you call a brain. You have the arrogance to come into this house almost uninvited and expect to beat me around the head with a verbal baseball bat and refuse to give me a chance to explain something which is as basic to me as the fact that we both have noses on our faces."

"That's bullshit!" An infuriated Bert was determined to impose his thinking on his brother. Maureen looked at her sister-in-law, hoping she could perhaps pour some oil on troubled waters.

Moira obliged. "No, what's bullshit, is the way you're reacting. You can take it from me as surely as I sit here that Bert Dempster is no longer welcome in this home until some time when you've demonstrated that you have something to reason with between your ears. Everyone who knows about this has rallied around, including our children and my father. If something wasn't done about Jack's condition it might have been a funeral you were attending instead of visiting us here and abusing us in our own home. Jack doesn't have to take it and, for damned sure, I'm not taking it. It's obvious that trying to give a fair and factual explanation is not going to happen today."

Maureen had said nothing after the initial greetings had been exchanged. Things were so hot and heavy that she saw discretion as the better way for her, but Moira was not about to let her get off lightly. "Maureen, I'm sorry for you. I sure hope this isn't the way your husband behaves when other things upset him. I can see what has happened. Hugh Dempster discussed it with you both but, as he's a man of limited vision when it comes to anything that requires a slightly more liberal view of things, it can hardly be said he would be the best one to give a full explanation. You can bet he'll be hearing more on this from us."

Bert spoke up moderating his tone somewhat. "Okay, okay, I understand where you're coming from, but there's no need to give the old man a bad time. Maybe I did come around here looking for a fight. In spite of whatever you've said, I don't like it one little bit."

"Okay, that's your choice," said Jack. "The person who has the most to lose through this is Moira. She really does have something to beef about, as she's losing a husband before her very eyes. But she realizes that this isn't something I chose or wanted. Can't you understand that this is something I was born with?"

Bert moved to interrupt. "Shut up, Bert. You've done enough damage and said far too much already," Maureen almost screamed at her husband. "I want to hear what Jack has to say. Can't you see that this might be our last chance? You're worse than a kid playing with matches around the propane stove. Keep on like this and it'll blow up in your face."

This seemed to get through to Bert. Resignedly he said, "Go ahead then, I'll try not to interrupt."

Jack gave them the whole story so far and what he expected for the future. Things were helped a bit as the result of Moira quietly pouring drinks for everyone. Bert's attitude seemed to soften and occasionally he even laughed at the odd thing that Jack said which struck him as humourous. At the end of it all Bert said, "I'm not wholly convinced, which I realize is my problem, not yours. However, you'll have to give us time to get used to it and you need not retaliate against the old man. He only has a limited understanding of it. He wasn't angry about it and he did try to give us a fair explanation of it. But remember this Jack, you and I were inseparable when we were kids and I always looked up to you as the older of the two of us. You've always been something of an icon to me and now I'm losing that. I guess that's as good a reason as I can think of for my anger. I apologize for that."

"Of course, I understand that very well, but let me remind you that you only have to get used to it. You don't live with me. You only come into contact with me on visits like this. In my case I have to reshape my entire life from top to bottom, almost from beginning to end. Just remember that, Bert. It might help you understand how little you're touched by this and how totally I'm affected."

* * * * *

Moira gave a lot of thought to the events of the past couple of weeks. Linda's visit had been most interesting. At last she had met another transsexual and she admitted to herself that she found her most likable and attractive. A short time ago Jack had told her that Linda's sexual drive favoured heterosexual men. Over a big part of her life, characterized as a gay man, she had suffered frustration and aggravation as she found little that appealed to her in gay men. Boy, that was some conundrum! She could understand why Linda had taken positive steps to unravel her complex life. By becoming a woman she could now pursue a relatively normal life with a heterosexual man.

What about Jackie, thought Moira. He had been a heterosexual man. Would he now turn over completely and become a heterosexual woman projecting her sexuality towards heterosexual men? Dr. Myers had indicated that, while this might be a textbook ideal, the reality could fall far short of this. According to the doctor, a great many straight transsexual men did not lose their preference for women when they became women.

Somehow she felt that a latent attraction was already felt by Jackie towards Linda and it might become gradually much stronger. But if Linda wanted a man she could not see the likelihood of a deeper relationship developing between them. On the other hand, in spite of Linda's obvious attractiveness, she had evidently not found a man. She knew that the average man, attracted to a woman, would be put off if he found that the subject of his affections was not a biological woman. This was one of the contradictions of transsexualism and being a contradiction it was also an inescapable trap for the average transsexual who had dreams of a beautiful romantic life with the man of her dreams. For many it would simply not happen.

Moira's thoughts turned to the Dempster family. She could understand Hugh Dempster failing to grasp the full dimensions of Jackie's problem. To put the burden of explanation on to Hugh's shoulders was about on a par with the blind leading the blind. As her thoughts turned to Bert Dempster she felt less charitable. She had always found Jackie's brother to be stiff and quite militaristic in his attitude. In fact there was often something about policemen which always identified them even when they were out of uniform. Some police had a well-known lack of sensitivity when it came to unfortunates, like transsexuals. She had discussed this by phone with Jackie's sister, Marion, after Bert and Maureen's visit. Marion had indicated that she would call Bert and lay out some facts for him.

What caused Moira to lapse into her current mood of deep thought was a phone call she had received about an hour before. It had been Marion to tell her that she had discussed the subject of Jackie's change with Bert and Maureen in a visit she had with them a few days ago. "He let me speak with little interruption. There was no show of temper. It was more a matter of resignation. I think that Maureen had been on to him quite a lot because he asked me why all the womenfolk supported Jack."

'"Maureen doesn't feel like I do about it," said Bert. "Moira seems to have handled it all in a very special way and even Mother is far more sympathetic to it than Dad is. It makes you think that the two sexes are in some sort of competition with each other, the women to make converts to their sex and the men to save another man from a fate worse than death." '

'"What's so wrong about being a woman?' I said. "You came out of a woman's womb. You're married to one and you have daughters. Is there something unnatural about all that, Bert?"

"No," he replied. "That's most natural. They were all born that way, just as I could have been born female with a slight change of circumstance. But I happen to think that it all becomes a matter of social ethics versus medical practices. I'm not particularly religious so I won't use the terms 'religious ethics,' that's why I prefer to say 'social'. There's a natural order to things and I don't believe it's for doctors to interfere. Nonetheless this is what they do. They psychoanalyse, feed hormones and then perform surgery to make a manufactured woman. That's all Jack can ever be."

Marion carried on, "So I put it to him. Would you stand in the way of Maureen having a hysterectomy if her doctor said it was necessary to save her life? It would be the end of bearing any more children and that, by your definition, would be interfering with the natural order. If you developed cataracts in your eyes and had them removed so you could see again, wouldn't that also not be interfering with the natural order?"

"I got an argument at this point. Then I put it to him that for years Jack had gone through a private hell over this, which might have led to his suicide. According to your reasoning, this had remained a matter of choice in Jack, that is until he committed suicide. Then you'd say that after all he must have really been off his head!" added Marion.

"You know, Moira, with the Berts of this world there's little that one can do or say. They have to reason it out for themselves. Bert's problem is that he's already in the first stage of grieving for the loss of an only brother and his reaction is to try to will it out of his life by total denial. It won't work, of course, but give him time and he'll eventually understand, I'm sure."

Moira returned to her musing. It was nice to have the intelligent support of Marion. The clear logic she presented was unarguable. But really, it wasn't Moira's problem. She could only do so much. If Jackie wished to do anything more about it, it was something she would have to handle herself. Moira's own response was to ignore Bert and that would be her advice to Jackie.

Chapter Ten

I Will Always Love You

The required two years on hormone treatment passed and Moira sat by Jacqueline's bedside waiting for her to recover from her anaesthetic. Her pale white skin now with beard growth removed by electrolysis, and long black hair spread on the pillow seemed unreal to Moira as she sat there patiently awaiting the return of her former husband, and now close friend, to the land of the conscious.

The clinic where the surgery was undertaken was in Montreal. Moira had an opportunity for a post-operative discussion with the surgeon. "Everything went very well, Mrs. Dempster, and she'll make a good recovery."

"Good, I'm relieved to know that."

"Can I make a personal observation?" asked the surgeon. Moira nodded her response.

"I think it's pretty wonderful for Jackie that her former wife has accompanied her down here. That's something which doesn't happen often."

"Doctor, I don't mind at all. I'm a lawyer and deal with a succession of family and divorce problems in our practice. What people do to each other in the name of vengeance, getting even or scoring one upmanship points is beyond belief. What all this has taught me is that, although we're no longer husband and wife, what would have been gained by either party had we decided to crucify each other? Sure I was injured, but Jackie could've been scarred for life, deprived of making a living, afraid to meet any of her old associates and hated by her children and family members. Because I provided the leadership, my kids are now fully accepting, after getting over their first misgivings. Jackie's parents have accepted her, even though her father was shocked out of his skin when he first heard about it. Her brother who was very antagonized over it all has now reached some degree of understanding of his new sister. My father, a retired law professor, finds the whole subject thoroughly absorbing and has enjoyed many lengthy chats with Jackie and her friend Linda, much of it relating to a new study he's doing which he calls 'transsexual law.'"

"It sounds most civilized," said the surgeon. "I think we could all learn a great deal from your attitude, Mrs. Dempster."

"Oh, please don't call me 'Mrs'. I have reverted to my maiden name of Davidson since I went into practice," Moira laughed.

"That's interesting. Are you both still living together?" commented the surgeon.

"Yes, we are. We're living together as good friends in a house we jointly own, but we don't sleep together. It's all a very friendly understanding. Jackie has retained her partnership in her consulting engineering firm and still presents papers and does most of what she used to do, but now she has additional responsibility for the female staff, which I guess is appropriate. She has been totally honest with everyone and most people seem to appreciate that because they don't like to feel hoodwinked. Some of her partners weren't happy about it when they first heard of it from the senior partner, with whom Jackie had some private discussions beforehand.

"She was still Jack when we went in to explain our situation almost two years ago. In fact, if the senior partner, John Haliburton, had said 'we can't handle it' they would have probably all supported him. But in his own craggy way looking a bit like Spencer Tracey, bless his heart, he growled, 'Jack, you'll still have the same brain won't you, and it's not being operated on is it?'

"Jack, as he was then, replied, 'Yes, I will John, and no, they will not be touching my brain.' With that John got up from behind his desk walked over and gave me a kiss, and shook Jack's hand.

"He said, 'If you were a woman now Jack, I'd have given you a kiss too, but don't you two worry. We're going to work this out to suit everyone and no one is going to resign.' He has been as good as his word. The opposition, such as it was, seems to have melted away. I think the final test came when Jackie delivered a paper to an international conference in San Francisco. She handled it brilliantly. She told them before she started that many of them knew her as the former Jack Dempster, so right away that cut down on the whispers and speculation."

"That's wonderful, but what about your parents?"

"My father has given us both much wise advice. Jack's father, a retired R.C.M.P. officer, a fighter pilot from the Second World War and twice decorated for valour, was aghast. I thought he was going to have a heart attack at first. He was so angry to think that his son could let the side down.

"He said, 'Damn it, Jack, an officer and gentleman just doesn't do these sort of things. You never gave any hint of this, what the hell are you thinking of?'

"Of course Jack was never an officer. I think what brought him around was when I held Jack's hand to signify our unity and both of our children came back into the room at the right time.

"Jennifer said, 'It's okay Grandpa, we're all behind Daddy in this thing.'

"Grandmother didn't have too much to say until they were leaving. 'Well goodbye, Jack and Moira. I hope you can work this all out. I think you can if you both show love and wisdom.' Turning to her husband she said, 'Hugh, quit worrying. It's all going to work out for the best.'

"Hugh Dempster went as red as a beetroot and could only say, 'Damn it, Beatrice, I never thought I'd ever live to see anything so bloody preposterous.'"

Moira was enjoying telling her tale, possibly because the doctor seemed fascinated by it all. He stood up and glanced at his watch. "I was so struck by your story that I quite lost track of time. Anyway, Ms. Davidson, good luck to you both," he said as they shook hands.

* * * * *

Jackie regained consciousness to see Moira sitting by the bed reading a book and waiting patiently. She reached her arm out and laid her hand gently on Moira's forearm. "Hello, darling, I guess you could say that this is the first day of my new life."

"And this will be the first kiss you've had on the first day of your new life," replied Moira as she leaned over and planted a kiss on Jackie's dry lips.

When they arrived back home at the airport they were welcomed by their two children. Jackie was very tired and could only think of bed as Jennifer drove the family car. All of them tried to up date each other on the latest family news and developments.

"Gran wants to have all of us over this weekend, including Grandpa Davidson. She's also invited Aunt Marion and your friend Linda, Dad, I mean, Jackie," Jennifer hastily corrected herself. Grandpa has promised to get his best Scotch whisky out."

"Wow, it sounds like it's going to be some party, particularly if Grandpa is going to get the Scotch out," replied Jackie, beaming with happiness.

What an interesting occasion that turned out to be for Jackie, now resplendent in a new dress specially purchased for the occasion for her by Moira and Linda. In a combination of red and black she looked spectacular with her dark hair swept back and with a make-up job supervised by Linda. Jennifer and Joshua agreed with their grandmother that "Dad, really looks like quite a beautiful lady."

Their grandfather growled, "What do you mean you two, she really is a beautiful lady and just try to remember not to call her Dad. She's Jackie now." He sounded almost proud as his new daughter came within earshot.

Linda and Moira were chatting with Moira's father, who found Linda's history as fascinating as that of his former son-in-law. He discussed the paper he was considering, dealing with Canadian law, and the need to better codify it as it applied to transsexuals. "Watching Jackie's problems and progress, and hearing more about yourself, Linda, has brought home to me the great need for a project like this."

* * * * *

The phone rang in the Dempster home. Moira languidly reached for it, having being awakened from a dozing session in front of the television.

The voice at the other end sounded familiar, but Moira couldn't place it immediately.

"Hello. Is that Mrs. Dempster?"

"Yes, indeed. Who's this?"

"Kathy Rakewood. Y'know, we usually run into each other at the supermarket."

"Of course. I knew the voice was familiar, but I'd dozed off when the phone rang so I needed a moment or two to become fully conscious."

"May I call you Moira, by the way? Please call me Kathy. The reason I'm phoning is that I heard through the jungle telegraph about your husband's sexchange and how you have both successfully handled it and your relationship. I hardly need ask if you have heard about David, my husband, and his tragic story?"

"Yes, I followed it like everyone else, no doubt. I'm truly sorry about it," replied Moira remembering that she had sent a card of condolence and wondering where this conversation was going to lead.

"I would really like to have a chat with you, Moira. I'm not quite sure why, as it's not a matter of crying over spilled milk. What has been done can't be undone," said Kathy.

"Well, yes, I suppose there's no reason why not. What did you have in mind?"

"I was wondering if we could get together for lunch."

Some days later Moira and Kathy Rakewood met at a local west side restaurant conveniently close to Moira's law office. They selected a table where they were unlikely to be overheard.

"It's good of you to give me the time, Moira. From what I hear from admiring friends of yours, the Simpsons and Guthries, the way you've handled and helped your husband to make the transition from Jack to Jacqueline has been a textbook example of how to do, and what to avoid, in handling a most difficult personal and family situation. I'm sure you'll appreciate that I haven't asked you to lunch for the purpose of bringing back old memories of a tragic period in my family life. On the other hand you can't talk about a subject like this without it coming up again."

Moira nodded agreement as she gave her attention to what sounded like Kathy's confession coming up.

"What David's death has left me with is the challenge of dealing with two children for whom the whole event has been gravely disturbing. I need to talk to another parent who has had similar exposures in a similar situation. I feel I can't talk to yet another psychiatrist. I know they mean well and have the academic know-how, but they seem to lack actual hands-on experience. At least they haven't lived this experience. It's easy enough to say you should or shouldn't do a certain thing, but they seem to overlook that we all have different personalities which help or distort our judgement."

"What's happened to bring you to this point then?" asked Moira now sensing that things had gone badly wrong for the Rakewood children.

"At the time of David's death our daughter Elaine, the older of the two, had been trying really hard to understand and get a grip on her relationship with her father. Of the three of us she was the one who consistently refused to condemn her father. I regret to say she showed a lot more wisdom than I did. When I refused to take any other position than one of total denial she was the one who insisted that there was a great deal more to her father's problem than simply having become an alcoholic. She used to say that both David and myself were running away from the same problem, he by drowning his sorrows in the bottle, and me by pretending that everything would be okay again if he would merely renounce his desire to be a woman. She was completely right, of course, and when David died she really went on the offensive."

Moira could say little and nodded her head sympathetically as Kathy continued to bare her soul.

"Until after the results of the inquiry, I steadfastly took the position that David had brought his problems upon himself. In retrospect that was very unwise. I wouldn't recognize what is widely understood as being the cause of transsexualism. If I had just accepted that it was a natural, but abnormal condition and not something he caught from someone else, it would've been a good start and would have encouraged him to deal with himself more positively. I know now that there was no way it would go away like a bad dream."

"When you said Elaine went on the offensive, what exactly did you mean?" asked Moira.

"Aided and abetted by my sister-in-law, Elizabeth Sadler, who I know you know, Elaine made a big effort to contact all our family and close friends to 'straighten them out' as she put it. She really got up the noses of quite a few people who did not want to hear 'the truth according to Elaine,' but the truth it was. Gradually, after following me and my highly biased explanations some of these people started to see the light and, in all honesty, it has badly bruised some of my friendships. I was very bitter about it, but in the end I had to recognize that Elaine was right. Worse still it also deteriorated my relationship with my younger child, Alan. If Elaine was her father's daughter then Alan is very much my son. When Alan turned against me, that was a cruel blow. I started at last to really face the truth."

Kathy had to excuse herself while she retreated to the ladies' room. Moira was left with her thoughts, forming a picture of a family which took sides, divided down the middle. Even after David's death and certainly up to the coroner's enquiry some two or more years ago, Kathy was fighting a rear guard battle trying to convince herself and others that she was right when it was never really a question of right or wrong. Clearly it was a matter of David's health. Instead, she insisted that her husband was so grossly perverted that if he wanted to turn off the spigot he could have done so, just like that. It was also a matter of David's dignity. She would rather have seen him destroy himself with alcohol than admit that she was wrong and that there was a role for humanity and compassion. Moira wondered how Kathy would take the news that her daughter Elaine, was dating Jeremy Dempster, drug addict and convicted felon.

Kathy returned and as soon as she was reseated Moira asked her, "What happened when Alan turned against you, Kathy?"

"Well, we had a heck of a row one day. He put it to me with the question as to what I'd do if he also turned out to be transsexual or maybe gay? I practically choked on the idea, but he said

I should start to think about things a little deeper and forget all my snobbish ideas about the 'right' things to do. At first he refused to say if he was gay or transsexual. He wanted to frighten me into seeing some reality and he succeeded. He tells me he's neither transsexual or gay and I have to take his word for that, but he did warn me to think instead of sticking my head in the sand. He said I should just remember it can happen to anyone, in any family and even the guy living next door or the girl across the street could be affected by something I, or polite society, would not approve of."

"Alan was right of course," Moira responded quietly. "A few minutes ago you mentioned that Elaine was aided and abetted by Elizabeth Sadler, who is, I should remind you a friend of ours. I'm aware that she's David's sister. I also know that you and she were involved in a well-known drink throwing scene when each of you threw drinks in the other's face. What was all that about, Kathy?"

Kathy bridled momentarily. "I think we both traded insults as there has never been much of a relationship between us. One thing led to another. I threw my drink at her and she replied immediately by doing the same."

"I heard of the incident, of course, from Elizabeth the day after it happened," said Moira. "According to the way I heard it, it had to do with the family seating arrangements at the church. Elizabeth, as the dead man's sister, felt snubbed and believed that you arranged things as a deliberate affront to the Rakewood side of the family."

Kathy coloured up with embarrassment. "I'm not proud of that. It just seems to be another in a long succession of stupid thoughtless acts for which it seems I'm well-known."

Moira did not respond further to that statement, although she silently agreed with Kathy's self-deprecating remark. She decided to change the subject when she asked, "How can I help?"

"I'm uncertain of that. I'm not sure that anyone can help me. I guess I mostly need a knowledgeable person to talk to who has been through the same experience as me, but has handled it all differently and a whole lot better. I'm having to figure things out as I go. I've been forced to recognize that I've lots of shortcomings and weaknesses of my own to surmount.

"But it's my kids who concern me most. I'm afraid that Elaine has become completely antagonistic towards me and clearly blames me for everything, except for the fact that David was born transsexual. I was unable to acknowledge the mistakes I made in handling and helping David until after his death when, in effect, Dr. Myers read the Riot Act to me and gave me a shaking up like I'd never known before. Among other things it brought home to me just how selfish and self-centred I'd become. On top of all that the position of Elaine and then Alan, became well known to me. Elaine went on the attack from the moment of learning of David's death and then Alan came at me from a different angle. He'd been told of all the sordid detail that came out at the inquest, being shown a transcript of it by Elaine. He'd known nothing of his father's transsexualism until then. He thought alcohol had been the sole problem, but after Elaine's intervention there was little he did not know. He's fond of the Sadlers and in turn he is clearly their favourite. He made it clear that I was at fault for the poor relationship with Elizabeth in particular and also that I contributed in a very tangible way to his father's death. And y'know, he may well be right."

"I don't know you well, Kathy, and I don't know your children at all, but for what it's worth, Jack, as she was then, and myself told our two about it together. More than that, we sat with each other on the chesterfield and held hands while telling them and we told them the complete truth. It took most of an evening of explanation and debate to have them both understand. Jack wanted to preserve his relationship with all of us and, above all, I wanted to hold the family together as a unit without excluding anyone, least of all Jack. Joshua needed special help because of the bonding between father and son. Jeremy our oldest son was in prison at the time, but when he came out, sobered up, we told him as gently as possible. They all felt some sense of bereavement, but we helped them over that. That's why it worked well for us in spite of all the hurdles we had ahead of us. When we went before the partnership at his firm I went with him and again held his hand as a token of our unity and it worked. When he went for surgery I also went with him. But there's something you must understand which goes beyond this."

"Oh, what's that?" asked Kathy expectantly.

"I never pushed him to do anything. Every move he made was his decision freely made and when he'd made it I stood behind him. His father was ready for a severe confrontation, but with the kids and myself clearly in support it just withered on the vine. There were a few hard words at first, but when Hugh Dempster could see that Jack had the support of his family he just became a big pussy cat."

"Jack also has two sisters and a brother and each presented a different reaction. The youngest sister, Marion, is a highly qualified nurse who knows quite a lot about gender dysphoria in her professional capacity. When told she became an instant ally. She had a professional knowledge of what Jack had gone through. His only brother, Bert, is a policeman and as it turned out he was a dyed-in-the-wool rejectionist. He could see nothing but the bad side of all this and made it clear that not only had Jack gone off his head, but had also embraced the worst aspects of perversion. We are not in touch very often with the eldest sister and her husband, a high school principal in Northern B.C., but fortunately she spoke to Marion first and got an accurate third party explanation of it all. Then she phoned us and assured Jackie of their support.

"But you didn't really fight for your marriage. Don't you think you made it too easy for him?" asked Kathy.

"I suppose you could say that, but to do anything else might have been a case of flogging a dead horse. Fighting for what? Satisfaction over holding the upper hand, that's what it would have been and what would the winning hand have held? Only the ashes of a marriage that had been killed rather than one that had been sensibly wound down? No, it was far better to face the truth and for everybody involved to come together in complete honesty. Denial is not facing the truth. Denial is like trying to turn the tide back like the legend of King Canute."

Moira continued, "You see, I had taken the early step of finding out as much as I could about it all before we got into the real crisis mode. I saw Dr. Myers, who clearly and patiently explained as much as she could about it. Then I went to the library and got some reliable books out. I did what every good lawyer should do and assembled the facts to avoid sticking my foot in my mouth. I knew enough to know that this was no light-hearted excursion into cross-dressing." Moira paused to take a drink from her wine glass.

"I had a few warning signals including when the full story of your David's inquest came out in the press. Jack was terribly upset, going as white as a sheet and retreating to the bathroom for a spell. What happened then I'm not sure, but I think he threw up. Even then he didn't tell me. Later, I found out when I read the paper. Sure, when he did come clean about his problem it was as if an earthquake had struck, but I stayed calm enough to think it out. After he blurted it all out, I knew our marriage would sink, but when I had time to think it all through later, I thought, why accompany it with as much destruction as possible. We haven't destroyed our marriage in any blind and thoughtless act of revenge. We have gently dismantled it. As a result we remain the best of friends and in our own special way we still love each other. I'm likely to marry again and Jackie fully accepts that."

"God, you've certainly handled it all in a most civilized and sensible way. Jackie has shown a lot of trust and courage and you in turn have been most humane and compassionate. I wish I could have been like that. Maybe David would have been alive today handling his sexchange with the same common sense that Jackie has shown. I admire you both immensely. Have you got any advice you can give me?" asked Kathy

"It's hard to give advice in a matter like this which is so tied up with emotions and prejudices. Have you ever openly and freely admitted that you were wrong in your judgement of David, or to put it a little crudely, have your children had to beat it out of you? Even at this late date, if you could put aside your pride, which is a part of your personality, and bare your soul to your children it might be a place to start. Another thing you could do is make things up with Elizabeth Sadler. She had a close bonding with her brother David who, in many ways, became her surrogate father when their own father died while she was still quite young. It would be better if you could become friends instead of remaining enemies," suggested Moira who had seen Kathy's perverse nature showing through her words.

Kathy seemed a little flustered as she groped for a reply. It wouldn't come. She broke down in tears. Moira felt uncomfortable as she watched Kathy struggling with something which was hard to define. She had evidently struck a raw nerve.

"Moira," she stammered, "forgive the tears. Foolish and false pride has been my downfall for years. I don't know whether the damage can ever be undone. What I did to my husband was stupid and unforgivable and my inability to face the truth has caused great problems for the relationship between the kids and me and with my in-laws. Can you help us?" It was a cry from the heart.

Moira pondered this sudden turn of events. She thought, 'I'm a lawyer in family practice. Doesn't my role include necessary counselling?'

She felt torn between her professional obligations and the need to help someone who was obviously in great distress.

"Kathy, I can help you, but on one condition. I'm in family practice and I can't be dispensing favours on the side. My obligations to my associates won't allow that. If you wish to see me as a professional advisor that's okay, but I'll also have to see and deal with your children. Also don't rule out the possibility that one or both might need some form of therapeutic counselling.

"The thing for you to keep in mind is reshaping your own attitude. It has to be said that you were aggressively destructive while David was alive, and ever since his death it seems to me that you've been fighting a rear guard action. I firmly believe that from here on you have to look at your actions and attitude as being constructive and rehabilitative. No one is going to condemn you for admitting you were wrong, in fact they'll probably come to admire you. Most people appreciate openness and honesty in dealing with problems. That's always a better option than half truths, smoke screens and admissions that have to be dragged out of a person," replied Moira.

Kathy looked relieved and Moira wondered why. These were heavy hits she had been handing to Kathy who, in spite of breaking down with the one brief bout of tears, seemed to draw inspiration from them. Then she realized that what Kathy wanted all along was someone to help her steer her course. Someone who would tell her the unvarnished truth. Someone who would not hold back merely because she was the wealthy and sometimes arrogant Kathy Rakewood. Maybe in this discussion Kathy had at last found the formula for her own solution to her life.

When Kathy spoke next, Moira knew that she had hit the nail on the head. "Oh, I now understand that perfectly. Don't worry about a fee. I'd expect that in any event. I've really brought a great deal of this on myself with my selfish, arrogant ways. It'll be worth anything to get this burden off my back and start to feel as though I have a life to live again."

* * * * *

Later, when at home with her own family, Moira talked of her meeting with Kathy Rakewood and the fact she was now a client of Moira's law practice. "However, Jeremy, I debated with myself about your relationship with Elaine and wondered if I should mention it to her mother who clearly had no knowledge of it. In the end I decided not to mention it as it is not my right to interfere in your affairs. The responsibility for that lays with Elaine."

"Yes, we've discussed it and Elaine intends to tell her mother. We have nothing to hide and we are both over 21, so it's up to us, I guess. We expect a bad reaction at first on account of my drug habit and prison record, but as Elaine says she would never go out with or marry some stuck up rich kid to please her mother. Elaine is of the earth and the sea, not fancy drawing rooms and china tea services. She was left a legacy by her father, so she is using that to complete her education and not spending it on fancy cars and clothing. Can I bring her around to meet you?"

"Yes, we'll be delighted," replied Moira.

* * * * *

Clive Jenkins was an unusual combination of vocations and talents. He was a friend of Captain Stephen Jones having worked on the street as a spiritual counsellor concentrating on youth problems, alcoholism and drug addiction. Through Stephen, he had also come to know Jeremy Dempster and had even participated in some counselling sessions. Captain Jones was well known for his tough love approach and while his clients seldom came to love him, they developed a profound respect for him.

Clive had a different tactic. His spiritual approach was not based on any one branch of the Christian religion, but was offered on a broad appreciation of God and the teachings of Christ without specific bias. His was a very low key ministry that relied to a great extent for its success in finding the better side of people and building upon it. Clive had come to the big city some years ago as a tall rangy cowboy from the bush somewhere around Alexis Creek. He had also worked in the Bralorne gold mine near Gold Bridge, an old gold mining area. He had his bout with alcohol and drugs and knew the destructive nature of both from personal experience and was thus able to help his clients based on this fact. However, the man who saved him from himself was none other than Stephen Jones and from that a firm friendship developed over the years between Stephen and Clive.

Clive of course had known of Jackie's gender change almost from their first meeting with the clergymen over two years ago. He had also met Jackie on many occasions as the two collaborated closely in making Clive's dream of a wilderness camp a reality. He was so used to Jackie that he learned to forget her past and had come to regard her as a close woman friend who he respected and admired, for her professional skills and always strong sense of integrity.

Stephen had also known of Jackie's gender change before it happened, having been told about it by Moira in her simple, direct way of addressing the subject. He had given Jeremy a lift from the tugboat company's dock to their home and had been invited to stay for an afternoon cup of tea or coffee. Steven was shocked at first and was immediately concerned about the wellbeing of the family and the possible effect this would have on Jeremy.

"Relax Steve, there's nothing for you to be concerned about. All the family knows including Jeremy, who was relieved to hear that there was someone in the family, like himself, who was less than perfect. His two younger siblings are diligent students, Jack is a prominent engineer and I'm a lawyer, and so it goes on throughout the family on both sides. The poor kid was labouring under a severe load of inferiority complex and running away, hence falling into the trap of drugs. Since he's known of Jack's plans he's been very supportive and it seems has become more reliable."

Steve accepted the position with Jack and after some consideration as they talked he said, "Don't worry about me Moira, it won't make any difference in my regard for Jack and working with him, or her, when this all happens. It's really none of my business and if I seemed shocked at first it was as if someone had just mugged me and I was struggling to get a hold on conscious reality. Now you've told me all the facts, I won't have any problem with it."

Clive's legacy was an area of bushland of about 160 acres of which about forty had been cleared and was in grass. Originally it had been crown land which Clive's parents had pre-empted and worked to eventually earn the deeds to the land. Described in the tax records as a farm, the land had been grazed by a neighbouring farmer who also took off a couple of crops of hay each season. This activity enabled Clive to keep the taxes at the lower farm rate. The other 120 acres was in lodge pole pine, through which a creek flowed. The creek reduced to a trickle in the dry season, but a deep drilled well placed there originally by Clive's father gave sufficient water flow when pumped with a lever type hand pump. Needless to say there was neither electric supply or telephone to the remote property, but it was connected by a dirt road of some seven miles to a blacktop highway.

Clive had tried to sell it in the past, but because of its remoteness there was little interest unless it could be nearly stolen. Gradually as his experience grew, he realized that this land could be an ideal site for building his wilderness camp which could cater to people who wanted to deal with addiction problems. He promoted the idea of a recovery camp and had actually got it going as a seasonal venture in a small way, but the place needed considerable improvements like a better water system and a small scale hydro generating plant to take advantage of the abundant water from the creek that ran through the property.

"Sounds goofy to say it, but Jackie is actually Jeremy Dempster's father and through working on Jeremy's problems I've come to know the family very well, particularly Jackie and they're very nice people," said Stephen.

"Yes, I know of her sexchange. She told me about it in an early meeting we had. In fact Jeremy and I have discussed it and we both agree that if that was what was needed in his father's case then so be it," replied Clive.

Clive thought back to the first time he actually met Jackie in her new mode. He had made an appointment to visit Jackie in her office, but was hardly prepared for the attractive well-dressed business executive who stood to greet him as he was ushered into her office.

"Jack this is a pleasurable surprise. Should I call you Ms. Dempster from now on, or can it be Jackie?" He asked in an easy, mischievous manner.

"Clive, to you I'm Jackie of course. I've come a long way since we had that first luncheon and I told you of my plans and then we went up one weekend to see your property. Just a couple of guys who drank a few beers coming and going. I remember it well."

"I've heard all about you from Stephen and Jeremy, but neither prepared me for the handsome woman I see in front of me. I take it you're now very happy with your life?."

"Yes, things have gone very well. Not just for me, but for my whole family given the circumstances."

They talked for a few minutes about the church group called together by Rev. George Marley. As a group, it grew at first with parents and other religious organizations taking an interest. It did not progress very far beyond that as factional groups started to split apart and form their own ideas of what they considered was suitable for their church. Nonetheless the three Protestant main-line churches continued to support the idea of a cooperative effort to help people and saw Clive's wilderness camp as one answer to their fight to stamp out drug addiction among their middle-class congregations. George Marley was a tower of strength gaining much support from Herbert Fawcett from the Anglicans and Hubert Schimmell of the Lutherans.

Clive spoke of his hopes for his project and spread some maps around to help his description. "We don't have a huge exchequer, but we do have a camp and if it's to grow we must improve both the power supply and the water system. We have a good year round creek flowing through the property and I think a Pelton wheel generator will give us all the power we need year round. Mind you the creek tends to get very low in the dry season, so a dam to provide water for the wheel will likely be needed."

"That should be fairly easy if the water is there and there is a good fall to it. The same water that turns the wheel can be used again if need be, run back into the creek or used for irrigation. Has the creek ever been assessed for its minimum water flow?" asked Jackie.

"No, but as it comes off a fairly high range about 5,000 feet high, it carries a good flow year round except in the dry spells replied Clive. "I'd guess maybe a 1,000 gallons per minute."

"Good. It sounds like a project that our firm could easily handle. Obviously we'd need to see it again and do a complete site and topographical survey, that would be the first step leading to a proposal. On the face of it and as I remember it, it doesn't sound complicated and if most of the material can be found on or near the site it shouldn't be too expensive either. What have you got up there already in terms of equipment or facilities?"

"We've got two bunkhouses that came from one of the mine properties and the original house which you've seen. That is my official residence and I've kept it fully habitable. We've also got a D6 bulldozer, a backhoe and a dumptruck. All the equipment is old but remains serviceable." replied Clive.

"How do you get your power and water now?"

"From a well with a hand pump. Also we have a two-inch plastic pipe that is fed from the creek and a small Honda gas powered generator."

"Sounds interesting. When can we go and see the property again? This time I'll take some survey equipment and everything necessary for producing a preliminary map"

"Anytime that suits you if you can give me about a week's notice."

"Yes I'd need a week myself. What I'd like to do is take Jeremy when he comes of his shift on the tugs. He'd enjoy it, I'm sure and getting him out in the country will be as good for him as a trip at sea. We're always worried about him and the temptation of Main and Hastings."

After Clive had left, Jackie for the first time saw a man through a woman's eye. 'He's very attractive,' she thought to herself. 'I wonder what the future might hold,' she speculated inwardly. This was a new emotion for her.

Chapter Eleven

Camp Golden

By now, a couple of years year after surgery, Jackie was thoroughly at home in her new role. Her partnership in her engineering firm was doing well and a proposal to build a dam to create a small reservoir, instal a Pelton wheel to generate electricity, and layout a water system at Clive Jenkins camp in the Cariboo district had been accepted and built. Clive was tight for funds, but Jackie donated a significant amount of capital to cover the deficiency after Clive had agreed to deed the property over to a charitable non-profit society of which both Clive and herself became directors. They had named the society The Camp Golden Society and the camp itself simply became known as Camp Golden. It was a name chosen by Clive in memory of his early days in the Bralorne and Cariboo Gold Quartz gold mines.

Clive had a theological education and took the view that Camp Golden was a Christian camp, but without any specific denominational ties. The three supportive clergymen, the Reverends Marley, Fawcett and Schimmel were added to the board of directors and each helped as they could through a special collection box in their churches. The thrust of their message to their congregations was that Camp Golden "is helping children of our community deal with their drug related problems." Drug addiction was serious in many parts of the city that used to think that it only existed in the Downtown Eastside. The reality became that

Camp Golden welcomed all within its boundaries who had a drug problem and wanted to kick it. Naturally they had to be willing to be bound by typical rules.

The rules included the obvious, a total ban on drugs and alcohol, no smoking within any building and assigned work projects each according to his or her skills. A simple non-denominational religious program existed for those who wished to participate which most did. The quarters were to be kept scrupulously clean and the land was worked to allow the camp to be self-supporting on many basic food items. Many could not pay any board, others could and were expected to make a reasonable contribution for their stays. Some useful income came from a bed and breakfast accommodation and a small campground for overnight camper and trailer visitors. The small artificial lake that formed behind the dam was turned into an attractive trout fishing facility that also supplied the camp with fish.

Things were moving along very well until the news came of a death in the family. Hugh Dempster died after a long period of indifferent health. The funeral was the occasion for the usual display of RCMP full dress uniforms and mementos of Hugh's service including his cap riding on the coffin and his medals. Since the original meeting of over three years ago when Bert Dempster took Jack to task over his planned gender change, the two had not been in direct contact. All news of their activities had been via the parents or through sister Marion.

The funeral of Hugh was the first big event involving the entire Dempster family in some four or five years. Bert Dempster, now a sergeant in command of a contingent who formed a local police force for the town where they lived, had shunned any display of interest in Jackie's progress or affairs. However, his wife Maureen always sent a friendly Christmas card to let Jackie and Moira know they were not forgotten.

Jackie wondered how Bert would react, particularly when he saw her there with Clive Jenkins with whom she now had a romantic relationship. Maureen had worked on Bert beforehand, reminding him that no matter what resentment he felt towards his ex-brother, she was now legitimately a woman, would look and act like a woman and would be due all the courtesies normally bestowed on a woman and she was very emphatic, "I want no scenes". Bert took a non-committal attitude which clearly signified that he would pass judgement when he saw his new sister.

Moira attended with Moira's two youngest Jennifer and Joshua, along with Jennifer's fiance. Jeremy came with Elaine, his girl friend, and Jackie and Clive. Jeremy was very close to his father particularly after the drug episode and he had a good relationship with Clive. In his time off from tugboating he would spend a lot of it at Camp Golden helping Clive with construction. Otherwise, he made his home with Jackie and Moira, who now had their house on the market. This would probably be the last occasion for a big social event at their home. The fact that it was a mournful occasion only fitted with Moira and Jackie's sad view that the sale of the house they had both enjoyed for so many years would be going to new owners.

The two halves of Moira's and Jackie's family mixed together quite well as there had never been any animosity between them except for the spat between Jack and Bert. Moira and Jackie were engaged in conversation over a drink when Bert walked up to them. He took Moira's hand and planted a peck on her cheek. He then shook hands with Jackie but avoided the usual peck he gave to any of the other women. "My, you look great Jackie. I would never have thought it possible," said Bert as he stepped back a pace to give her a good appraising look. After an exchange of pleasantries Bert drew Jackie aside while Moira moved on feeling that the two might want a moment of privacy.

"I want to apologize for the way I treated you that day when Maureen and I came around to give you hell for changing sex. Aside from the fact that it was none of my business, I acted in a boorish, insensitive manner and you deserved far better for standing up all four square and dealing with your challenges. We all have challenges, but yours was as tough a one as anyone could ever visualize."

"That's very kind of you," replied Jackie. "I'm so glad to see we've broken the ice and hopefully can be friends again."

"I'd like that and I've heard other good things about you. You're still a highly respected professional engineer and seem to have only continued to grow in your profession. And then there's how you managed to steer Jeremy around his problems. We've met and spoken to him and his girl friend and they seem like a fine young couple and I gather he's doing quite well on the tugboats. He tells me he is going up for his mate's certificate later this year. I wish him every success."

"Yes, considering everything and the mess he was in a few years ago. Moira and I are very proud of him. Never in our wildest dreams would we have ever thought that one of our kids would become a tugboat man, but we don't care. He's in an honourable activity that he clearly enjoys and it's been a contributing factor in getting him away from the drug life to which we almost lost him. A lot of the credit for that is due to Stephen Jones over there and my friend Clive. Elaine's a social worker and they met when she was still a student doing a special assignment as part of her course. It must have been divine providence when she was allocated to him, because I gather the attraction took hold from the beginning. She's a bit of a rebel herself, being the daughter of David and Kathy Rakewood, and I gather she let it be known in no uncertain terms that she would never marry someone to meet her family's ideas of social acceptance alone."

The slight change in Jackie's tone of voice when she mentioned Clive, was not lost on Bert. "What's your relationship with Clive. Strictly business or more than that?" asked Bert, a trace mischievously.

"We're very fond of each other. It was all business at first, but when a man and a woman come into contact there is often a chemistry that develops between them. It's just one of the laws of nature. I guess that chemistry exists between Clive and me. He's a very good natured and loving man who's easy to be with and that's all I want. We can't have children for obvious reasons, so we pour our energies into Camp Golden. The people who come there from recovering alcoholics and druggies, and at different times, children's groups are all our children and then we also provide a bed and breakfast to passing people."

"Sounds great. Can Maureen and I visit it sometime? We love the interior, but I don't know that section too well."

"We'd love to have you," replied Jackie. "I plan on retiring from engineering in about five years time. Joshua will be through medical school, Jennifer is off our hands and Jeremy has ambitions to become a captain. We'll keep a smaller place in Vancouver, but Camp Golden will become our main home. Clive's house up there is what his parents left him, so it has been moved to a new site on the property and rebuilt as the main lodge in which we will live. Yes, do come and visit, but let us know a little ahead so we can get the concrete mixer out of the living room!"

Bert then said, "I should move along and mix a little." He leaned forward and placed his hand around the back of Jackie's neck and gave her a firm kiss on the cheek. It was symbolic of his acceptance of his sister and it did not go unnoticed by other members of the family.

"I noticed that kiss that Bert gave you," said sister Marion. "So far as Bert is concerned you're now back in the family as a full-fledged dues paying member of the clan."

Jackie giggled, "What d'you mean dues paying member. I've always paid my way in double time."

"Yeah, I know. What I mean is that you'll now be able to spread the welcome mat at wherever you're living and you should expect the same in return."

"Oh, okay. Bert has already invited Maureen and himself to visit Clive and me at Camp Golden, or to be fair, he asked if they could visit and I told him by all means. We're pretty proud of what has been achieved so far, but there's a lot more to do yet, like building a new guest cabin for the adult visitors."

Clive had not moved in with Jackie and would not, so long as Moira was there under the same roof. It was for no other reason than Jackie did not want to have Moira's boy friend move in and they had both agreed to maintain the status quo until the house was sold and they had both gone their separate ways.

* * * * *

During the next several weeks the house sold on a greatly inflated Vancouver real estate market and, by mutual agreement they split the proceeds of well over a million dollars. Living together as friends had been successful but, as Jackie always knew it was highly likely that a new man would enter the life of her former wife and when that happened she did not want to cramp her style. And now, of course, without any seeking out, a new man was taking up a good part of Jackie's life.

Jackie bought a comfortable condominium for herself and Linda moved in as a room mate. Moira married again to Phil Harrison another lawyer and Jackie and Clive attended the wedding. Jackie expressed her sadness to Clive, but readily acknowledged it was Moira's complete right and silently hoped that the same would happen for her and Clive someday. Phil knew all about Jackie and welcomed her and Clive into his family circle.

Moira stayed in touch with Kathy Rakewood who gradually recovered from her personal disaster, although Kathy's relationship with her children remained tense at times. Elaine, her daughter, and Alan, her son, went through considerable difficulties. Eventually Alan pulled himself together and joined the City Police Force, which was quite outside any ideas that the Rakewoods ever had for their son. Elaine forgave Kathy for what she regarded as gross negligence and cruelty in her mother's attitude and dealings with her father, David Rakewood. So long as Elaine was alive David Rakewood would never be forgotten.

When Kathy told Elaine that she was in love with a recovering drug addict with a criminal record, Kathy was livid to think that her daughter would demean herself in such a way. "What in hell are you thinking of Elaine. You're making a bed of thorns for yourself. With that to drag around you won't be very welcome among a great many people I know. To think you would humiliate us all in this way is disgusting." Elaine's face was red with anger but she quickly cooled down when Elaine replied to her.

"You don't even know who my guy is and yet you runaway at the mouth in your usual style, sticking your foot inside it at the same time. He is Jeremy Dempster, the son of your lawyer, your consultant and your confidante. The Dempster family have only gone through what a fair number of other well-to-do families from the West side have endured and they've handled it very well, so for that you have to give them credit. Jeremy is actually a very nice man and one I'm proud to feel I have helped in a significant way. Many people have hidden weaknesses which when they come out are found to be manageable if not completely curable. Jeremy's father is an example. My father could have been another. I personally am yet another."

"How were you affected? You're not an alcoholic or drug addict are you?" Kathy shot in.

"No I'm neither, but I was a hippie until Dad's death if you remember, embracing a runaway lifestyle, smoking grass and hash and aimlessly living like a tramp on the Pacific shore of Vancouver Island," said Elaine. "Now, I'm training for a worthwhile career helping others less fortunate. I met Jeremy when he was behind bars -- it was a course assignment. His condition was not good and his outlook on life very negative. Since then he's come a long way. He's been clean since he came out a couple of years ago. He has a good job with good prospects and I've come to love him very deeply as he loves me. We plan to spend the rest of our lives together. He is moving in with me in the next few days as we now consider we're engaged with the idea of marrying in the near future."

Elaine awaited her mother's reaction, expecting more nonsense. Instead Kathy remained silent while her face went white and then became very flushed. "Mum, are you okay. Why don't you sit down and I'll make a cup of tea." Elaine was afraid that Kathy might have a heart attack. "I'd like a cup of tea, but I'll be okay. My mind went in fast reverse to Dad's death and then it replayed all my mistakes of the years that followed as I was reminded of everything Moira taught me. No, Elaine I'm not going to attack or criticize. If Jeremy is who you want, that's fine with me. I'm glad you've found a man you can love. You're over 21 and can make up your own mind. Jeremy's mother has taught me a lot and I apologize for my brief outburst a few moments ago when you first mentioned your plans. I hope you'll forgive me and I look forward to meeting Jeremy."

"Thanks, Mum, that was nice."

* * * * *

Elaine and Jeremy had been intensely private about their relationship, but both were welcomed into the other's parents' homes and Elaine started to work with Clive and Cap'n Stephen Jones. Elaine travelled with Jeremy when he went up to Camp Golden and it was there in the privacy and quiet of the lodge that they were first able to consummate their love. It was a moment of joy for both as they lay there breathless with her head on his chest. Jeremy marvelled that he was were he was after coming so close to destruction. Elaine marvelled at the miracle of life as she could feel his heart pounding under her ear. It woke up her biological clock as she thought of the babies she and Jeremy would eventually parent and it was a feeling she had never let herself dwell upon in the past. At that moment life for both of them looked wonderful and very precious.

Eventually Kathy Rakewood met Jackie on a social occasion at Moira and Phil's home. It was to celebrate the formal announcement of Jeremy and Elaine's engagement. Kathy was impressed with the handsome woman who stood before her. Jackie and Kathy enjoyed a conversation with each other during which Kathy paid Jackie several compliments.

"I remember you as a pretty regular looking guy, but now that I've seen the new you in the flesh, you're not hard to take. In fact, you're a helluva sight better looking than a great many women your age. Y'know, I look at you now and think I'd give anything to see Dave standing before me, a happy healthy woman, rather than a suicidal alcoholic dying in a blazing wreck." She turned serious for a moment as she shuddered. "God, I think that scene will haunt me to the end of my days!"

Jackie was a little lost for words as she looked at this woman whose legendary beauty was clearly fading. "I guess there are some things you simply have to put behind you and get on with your life. It was a very sad occasion for you and your family, but life must go on."

"I'm pleased we're to become in-laws," Kathy said as she changed the subject. "It'll be good to know that we will be able to share grandparenting, but how would you handle who is to be the grandmother on your side?"

"Well, Moira and I were pretty thorough on that point. The two younger ones Jennifer and Joshua and, their future spouses, will have Phil and Moira as grandparents and I'll be a special aunt. In the case of Jeremy and Elaine, I'll be the grandmother and Moira the special aunt."

"God, I have to admire you Dempsters. You've been so sensible and yet so caring in every arrangement you've made. I wish I could have been so civilized. I guess that's why Moira has been such a huge help to me. Mind you I nearly put a fatal foot in it when Elaine told me of her affair with your Jeremy until I knew who he was. Fortunately, remembering the lessons learned from Moira, I was able to get my foot out of my mouth before any serious damage was done." Kathy grimaced as if retracing the foot in mouth scene.

They were joined by Elizabeth and Tom Sadler. Their rift with Kathy had been repaired through the intervention of Moira, who pointed out that this type of quarrel was without satisfaction or profit to either side. All that was ever gained was another dose of wounded pride and while Kathy and the Sadlers would never be bosom friends, they could now meet and be friendly to each other. Moira sometimes marvelled at how poorly equipped Kathy had been to deal with life. She was living proof that beauty and a fancy education at a girls' exclusive school, by itself was seldom enough. From a spoiled child Kathy had grown into a selfish woman, but gradually with Moira acting as her counsellor, she could see the error of her ways. Today it was a sadder but wiser Kathy, a woman who had now found compassion, forgiveness and genuine interest and concern for other people to be far more satisfying than the selfish self-centred Kathy of a few short years ago.

* * * * *

Jackie went to see Dr. Myers on her annual visitation to her clinic to tell her and Dr. Fellowes all about her experiences, including Moira's new marriage and her own relationship, which by now had become a marriage proposal. As the effects of the surgery took hold and the flow of all testosterone was removed, Jackie's natural femininity improved and by many she would have been regarded as being a rather beautiful middle-aged woman.

Dr. Fellowes asked who should take the most credit for the way things had worked out so successfully. Jackie replied, "There's no question, Moira of course. If she had gone against me it would have split the family. But with the stand she took and the leadership she provided it kept the family united in my support. She has married again and I just hope her new husband doesn't turn out to be a transsexual!"

They all had a laugh over that, "And are you happy now, Jackie? What about your personal life. You mustn't become some sort of hermit, you know," remarked Dr. Myers.

"Yes, things are going well. I'm healthy and I sleep well at night without being disturbed with endless anxiety. It's so good to get rid of all that old baggage and all the stress it created. Now that it's all behind me, I'm so settled in my role as Jacqueline that the old me, the male Jack Dempster, is becoming a memory who seems quite distant at times. At other times I think of him in a sort of affectionate way. I'm not that different now, but in the more obvious ways I'm a different person. Moira and I will soon be grandparents and this has kept us close as we have this new mutual interest. We've agreed that Phil, her husband, will be Grandpa to Jennifer's child, Moira will be Grandma and I will be a very special aunt. It sort of puts me in the second rank, but I accept that as a better alternative to any dissent over the matter. It'll be the other way when Jeremy has children."

"Do you have a man in your life?" asked Dr. Myers, her voice betraying her curiosity.

"Yes, I do. Clive Jenkins is my husband-to-be and both Jeremy and myself are very much a part of his camp project for helping drug addicts and inner city children. All our three children are doing well and Moira and I remain on the best of terms," concluded Jackie.

As the three parted company, both doctors agree that this was a very civilized and sensible arrangement. Later Margaret Myers remarked to her colleague, "You know, George, it always takes two to tango. When Jackie gave top credit to Moira, you no doubt noticed that she never referred to herself. In reality they were perfect partners for each other with what they had to contend with. It also needed Jackie's sense of loyalty, fair play and her dutiful regard and concern for her family to make it work as well as it did. It was Jack who shouldered the heaviest burden when he used to go down to skid row to find his son and keep the family contacts alive.

* * * * *

Jacqueline Dempster was the type of person who periodically stopped and counted her blessings, but sometimes it was an occasion when she had to fight self-doubt. To be certain, her life with Moira had wound down, but there was plenty remaining of mutual interest through their children. Jeremy would always be subject to a question mark, but in spite of this he was doing well, he had reacquired the ambition of his earlier years. He could now be trusted and the combination of the sea and the basics of the land at Camp Golden seemed to suit him very well. He had been driving his own car for some years now and had shaken the dependency on drugs completely. Better still it looked like he had a life partner who knew and understood his weaknesses and would give him strength.

Clive seemed to have given Jackie objectives in life which she had not experienced before. The dedication of both of them to Camp Golden gave Jackie an abundant outlet for her still considerable energies, but she thought to herself on a number of occasions, "Am I really a woman?" or was she still a man masquerading as a woman. These were moments when her self-confidence stalled like a car that could not quite make the top of the hill. She had been completely honest about her past to Clive and there was nothing he didn't know about her and her family, so why was she worrying?

At moments like these she would get in touch with Dr. Myers to "recharge her batteries" as she would describe her temporary need for rebuilding her confidence. At other times a good heart to heart talk with her friend Linda helped a great deal.

Linda always practical would say, "You're giving yourself to a man which is what most women do when they get married. That is the way in which mankind has progressed since the beginning of time, so accept the inevitable, Gal, unless you want to be an old maid living out your final years in loneliness and without the knowledge that you made a guy happy while it lasted."

"Is part of my nagging worry, the fact that I'm losing the sense of independence I enjoyed as a man?" asked Jackie.

"I suppose that may be true to a limited degree, but don't forget that few of us are independent in this life. Financial independence we may have, but that's not what I'm talking about. I'm talking about our need for interdependence with other people for their society. We all need friends, if we have good relatives and a strong family connection so much the better. For you and Clive coming together in love is better still, so count your blessings. You've got a good man there and don't forget he's giving up a lot of his independence for you as well. It's a matter of mutual support and I just wish I had it. Maybe the right man will come along, maybe he won't, but I'll cope with that as I always have."

Jackie paused for several moments as if gathering her thoughts. "You're right of course. I guess a lot of it has to do with adoption in later life of a whole new code for living with all the new social and emotional responses attached. It was never an easy task for any trans-person. There is one thing though I have to say. Linda we've been the best of friends. You gave me support when I most needed it and you give me support now. You've always been here for me and I hope I can always give you the same kind of support. You know you're really one of the family and you'll always be welcome at Camp Golden as you are here."

* * * * *

CAST OF CHARACTERS

AUSTIN	Harry	- Rakewood plant employee
AZZIZ	Mr.	- Muslim gentleman, client of Jack
BOWKER	Linda	- Insurance underwriter, friend of Jack
CARLO		- Mrs. Rakewood's hairdresser
COLLINS	Captain	- Tugboat master
DAVIDSON	Lyle	- Retired law professor. Father of Moira Dempster
DEMPSTER	Jack	- Central subject of story, husband of Moira. Later adopts name Jacqueline or Jackie
	Moira	- Wife of Jack
	Beatrice	- Mother of Jack
	Bert	- Brother of Jack
	Hugh	- Father of Jack
	Jennifer	- Daughter of Jack
	Jeremy	- Oldest son of Jack
	Joshua	- Younger son and youngest child of Jack
	Marion	- Younger sister of Jack
	Margaret	- Older sister of Jack, wife of Frank Frostad
	Maureen	- Wife of Bert Dempster

EARLY	Jake	- Rakewood plant employee
FAWCETT	Herbert	- Anglican Church minister
FELLOWES	Dr. George	- Partner in practice of Dr. Margaret Myers
FORBES	Joan	- Lawyer friend of Moira
GUTHRIE	Simon & Peggy	- Lawyer and wife
HALIBURTON	John	- Head of Engineering partnership
HARRISON	Phil	- Lawyer who becomes second husband of Moira Dempster
JENKINS	Clive	- Social worker and spiritual counsellor
JONES	Stephen	- Former sea captain and social worker
LEIGHTON	Sylvia	- Transsexual hooker. Befriender of David
MARLEY	George	- United Church minister
MELNICK	Doug	- Insurance company manager

MYERS	Margaret	-	Psychiatrist and leading specialist in sexual medicine
O'SULLY	Patrick	-	Catholic Church minister
RAKEWOOD	David	-	Husband of Kathy Rakewood and leading local industrialist
	Kathy	-	Wife of David
	Alan	-	Youngest child of David & Kathy
	Elaine	-	Eldest child of David & Kathy
RAKOSY	Theodore	-	Grandfather of David Rakewood and Elizabeth Sadler
ROYLE	Mr.	-	Assistant school headmaster
SADLER	Elizabeth	-	Sister of David Rakewood
	Tom	-	Her husband, and stock broker
SCHIMMELL	Hubert	-	Lutheran church minister
SIMPSON	Ben	-	Engineer partner of Jack Dempster

A Tale of Two Wives